JAMES DeVITA

BLUE

LAURA GERINGER BOOKS

An Imprint of HarperCollins*Publishers*

Library of Congress Cataloging-in-Publication Data
DeVita, James.
  Blue / James DeVita.
    p.   cm.
  Summary: Seeking freedom from his restrictive home and school life, Morgan,
using his own powers, becomes a magnificent fish—the blue marlin.
  ISBN 0-06-029545-7 — ISBN 0-06-029546-5 (lib. bdg.)
  [1. Marlins—Fiction. 2. Fishes—Fiction.] I. Title.
PZ7.D49827 Bl 2001   00-59706
[Fic]—dc21   CIP
                                                                      AC
Typography by Alicia Mikles and Jennifer Crilly
1 2 3 4 5 6 7 8 9 10
❖
First Edition

For my father
—J.D.

Among the many people who have helped me along the way with this book, I would particularly like to thank Mrs. Barbara Esbensen for her well-needed advice and encouragement when I first began this novel; Mr. Noel Silverman for his generosity, expertise, and friendship; my wife, Brenda Bedard, for her unflagging support, patience, and insightful criticism; and my parents, for their gift of the sea.

—*J.D.*

CHAPTER ONE

ORGAN HAD NEVER been in an ambulance before. It was smaller inside than he had imagined. His mother and two paramedics were in the back with him, Mrs. Pasalaqua was in the front seat with the driver, and his father was following in the family car. Lights were flashing, sirens were screaming, and Morgan just wished they'd all stop making such a big deal.

"What's your name?" asked one of the para-medics. He flicked a small penlight across Morgan's eyes. "Do you know your name?"

"That's a stupid question," Morgan thought. "Of course I know my name."

"Your name?" the man asked again, this time putting his hand in front of Morgan's face. "Okay, how many fingers am I holding up? What day of the week is it? Do you know what today is?"

"What's with these guys?" thought Morgan.

"C'mon, Morgan," said the other paramedic, "do you know where you are? Talk to us."

"Morgan? Morgan, honey, answer the man," his mother added.

Morgan tried to . . . but couldn't.

"Mmpghmmnghp" was all that came out. He tried to move his lips, but they wouldn't budge. "Mmpgghgmnp!" Still nothing. He couldn't open his mouth. He stretched his face and twisted his nose, dropped his chin, furrowed his brows, and pulled with all his might . . . but his lips wouldn't move.

"Stop making faces at the nice man, Morgan," snapped his mother.

"I'm not making faces, I can't open my mouth!" Morgan yelled, grabbing his mother's hand. But all that came out was "Aomn mou mghigh aieies, uaow ain ouwamm mm mmauoeu!"

The paramedic quickly leaned into Morgan with a puzzled look on his face. He reached across him, snatched up a tongue depressor, and aimed it at Morgan's mouth, but missed and stabbed the pillow as the ambulance swerved into the hospital parking lot and stopped with a sharp screech. The back doors were flung open, and the paramedics hurriedly began unclicking and reclacking all kinds of things. They rolled and bumped Morgan out of the ambulance and wheeled him across the parking lot. Morgan stared up at the night sky. The gurney popped a little wheelie as it thumped over a speed bump.

"This isn't a grocery cart, you know," Morgan thought, shooting the paramedic a look.

One more thump up a curb, and the stars disappeared from Morgan's view. The bright lights of the hospital loomed over him.

"Aiooioaiiouummphooieaiinuuaaiieeaae!" *(Why is everybody making such a big deal!)* he screamed.

The paramedics wheeled Morgan into the emergency room.

CHAPTER TWO

IT ALL STARTED about a week earlier, on a Sunday-like-any-other-Sunday in Morgan's house.

Ring!! rang his father's alarm clock at exactly six o'clock, just like it had every single morning for as long as Morgan could remember mornings.

Morgan scrunched himself into the corner of his bed and pulled a pillow around his ears, but he knew he would never get back to sleep. He listened to his father shower, shave, get dressed, and make enough noise to wake up half the neighborhood. At exactly six thirty-three he heard his father slam the front door on his way out of the apartment.

Morgan slid out of bed and wandered sleepily over to the front window in the living room. He flopped himself down in a chair and pressed his nose against the cold glass. It was raining.

Again. Morgan could see his father leaving the building three floors below. He watched him as his father pulled up the hood of his jacket and cinched it tight under his chin.

"Cigar," Morgan thought.

His father stopped at the bottom of the stoop and took out his Sunday cigar. He huddled over it, cupping his hands around a match, and tried to light it.

"I don't think so," Morgan said to himself.

His father threw the wet matches on the sidewalk and made his way across the street.

Morgan watched him walk down the block, hunched over and heavy, past the long rows of brick apartment buildings. They stretched on for as far as Morgan could see, up and down both sides of the block, each one exactly like the one next to it.

Morgan leaned against the window a bit more to get a better view of his father, who was at the newsstand now. Morgan stared blankly after him. His father bought a paper, tucked it under his coat, turned around, and took exactly the same route home again.

Morgan headed to the kitchen. His father came in smelling like rain smells, dumped the

Sunday paper on the table, and began to cook breakfast. Sunday was the only day of the week Morgan's father cooked anything. First he put his coffee on and tuned in the radio. Then he started on the bacon.

Morgan plopped down at the kitchen table, listening to what his father called music, and watched him cook. When the bacon was done, his father laid the pieces neatly side by side on a paper towel.

"Take away three," Morgan thought with a yawn.

His father placed exactly three strips on a different paper towel, wrapped them up, and stuck them up on top of the fridge.

"Surprise," Morgan said to himself, not surprised.

The bacon on top of the fridge was for Morgan's mother. She always got three pieces, Morgan got two plus some crumbly overcooked bits, and his father took the rest.

Frying pan still in hand, his father pushed some English muffins into the toaster and swung around to the window to dump the hot grease into the garbage bin three stories below. He waited for Morgan to join him. They both

6

poked their heads outside as his father slowly poured. They watched as the grease splashed into the Dumpster below with a smoky hiss.

They lingered there for a moment, half hanging out the window, the rain puddering softly on their heads, staring down. Morgan remembered how his father used to take him up on the roof to watch the older kids play stickball down on the street in front of their building. They'd both hang over the front ledge, kind of like they were doing now, and yell and scream and take sides and pretend they were at a real baseball game.

The wet air smelled good. Morgan looked over at his father.

"Hey, Dad," Morgan started to say, "what do you say we—"

"It's raining," his father said gruffly, shuffling back to the stove. "Close that, would you?"

Morgan closed the window halfway and plopped back down at the table. His father cracked three eggs into the frying pan.

"Now the paper and coffee. He's got about a minute and a half till the eggs are done," Morgan thought, glancing at the kitchen clock.

After pouring himself some coffee, his

father quickly culled through the newspaper, pulled out the sections he wanted to read, and threw the rest onto the chair next to him. He sharpened a pencil for the crossword, carefully positioned the best sections of the paper just the right distance to the left of his plate—making sure that the funnies were on top—spun around, and plucked the eggs off the stove.

"Amazing," Morgan mused.

Wielding a spatula, his father scooped up the eggs and gave himself one, Morgan one, and himself another. Then he swung back around to the sink and tossed in the pan. He poured a tiny splash of water into it, which crackled and sputtered in the still-hot grease, which cued the English muffins to pop up. Which they did. They always did. At the same moment every Sunday . . . pan in the sink, water, sputter, *pop!* Then he turned back to the table, juggling the hot muffins, and flung one to Morgan and one to himself, and *voilà!* Done! Time: 7:08 AM. Every Sunday. 7:08 AM.

His father was an accountant.

Morgan's mother came out of the bathroom wearing a pink fuzzy robe. Still half asleep, she reached up and grabbed her stash of bacon off the fridge. She pushed down an English muffin for herself, poured some coffee, and walked over to the window. She leaned against the wall and stared out, arms crossed, nibbling on a piece of the bacon, and waited for her muffin to pop.

Pop!

She slippered over to the counter and made herself a bacon sandwich, refilled her coffee, sat at the table, and started to read whatever pieces of the newspaper were left sitting on the chair.

Morgan tapped his fork and pushed his crumbly pieces of bacon around on his plate. His father turned a page of the paper. His mother buried her head in the coupon section.

"Somebody talk," Morgan thought.

He waited for what seemed like a week and was just about to slide off the front of his chair and disappear into a bored blob underneath the table when his mother finally spoke.

"I've got a lot to do today," she said to his father.

"It's raining," he answered, glancing up from behind his paper.

It sounded almost like a conversation . . . the words hung in the air for a moment . . . but then they both dove back into their papers.

"Argh," Morgan groaned to himself. "Can I have the funnies?"

"When I'm done," his father said, snatching them up. "Didn't I ask you to shut the window?"

"It feels good," Morgan answered.

"You're getting the floor all wet. Close it."

It was really raining hard now. Every so often a flash of lightning would brighten up the darkened city sky, and a few seconds later a grumble of thunder would catch up to it. The gutters on the roof were backed up, and the wind splashed off sheets of rain that waterfalled down to the alley below.

"Close it, Morgan," his mother added for emphasis.

Morgan got up and walked over to the window on his heels. He was trying to land each heel in the center of a different tile on the linoleum floor. He counted them as he went along. He lost his balance and went backward six tiles, sideways for three, and banged into the cupboard.

"Morgan James," his father said without looking up from the paper.

Morgan pushed himself off the cupboard

and righted himself, still on his heels. He leaned his weight forward and tried for the window again. He made it there without touching the edge of a single tile and closed it almost all the way. He left it open about two inches from the bottom.

Morgan stared out the window. Across the alley, he could see, another father was sitting at a kitchen table reading a paper.

"I'm done," Morgan said to his mother of his breakfast, and went into the living room. He flicked on the TV, spun around, and took a running leap from about three feet away into his father's easy chair.

"Morgan!" his father yelled from the kitchen.

"I fell!" Morgan yelled back, snuggling down into the noisy leather chair. It squeaked and made squishy air noises as Morgan burrowed into it. He stared his Sunday stare into the TV and waited for the commercial to end. Just then his father came into the room, changed the channel without asking, and ordered Morgan out of *his* chair.

His father plopped himself down with one loud swoosh.

"I give him fifteen minutes," Morgan estimated, sitting on the floor where he could see the clock. His father stared blankly at the TV—at the boob tube, as he called it, the black hole.

"This thing'll—*yawn*—suck your life away," his father said, staring at the screen all the same.

In exactly six minutes and twelve seconds Morgan's father fell fast asleep. He slumped a little farther down in his easy chair with each belabored breath. His arms drooped straight down, almost touching the floor, and his chin rested on his chest, which heaved up and down in funny little fits and starts.

"Under ten. Not bad," Morgan considered as he got up to change the channel. The moment his fingertips brushed the dial, his father sat bolt upright in his chair, eyes bugged out, and bellowed, "I'm watching that!"

Morgan wandered back into the kitchen and sat down next to his mother. He rolled a section of the Sunday paper lengthwise into a long tube and peered through it at his mother. She was clipping coupons.

"I'm really—*clip*—busy, Morgan. What do you want?"

"Nothing."

"Why don't you—*clip, clip*—go do something."

"This just in, Mom," he said through the rolled newspaper, using it like a megaphone. "It's *raining*! There *is* nothing to do!"

"Use your imagination."

"We don't have any in this house."

"Don't give me any of your sob stories, okay?" his mother said with a clip. "I could think of a million—stop playing with that—I could think of a million things you could do. Clean your room, put away your summer clothes, wash the dishes—"

Morgan blew through the rolled newspaper and scattered the coupons across the table.

"Morgan James!" his mother said, grabbing the newspaper away from him.

"I was using my imagination!" he said in his defense. "*Wind.* I was being the wind."

"Are you being smart with me?" his mother asked. "Are you!?"

"No," he assured her, lying. "No." Morgan helped his mother gather up the coupons. "Can I . . . can I have that back?" he asked penitently.

His mother gave him back the newspaper roll.

"Go find something to do," she added. "*Now*. And don't wake up your father."

Morgan moped back down the hall and peered into the living room with his rolled-up newspaper. Sure enough, his father was asleep again.

Quietly Morgan tiptoed toward the TV. He stood in front of it and slowly reached out his hand—

"I'm watching that!" yelled the easy chair.

"AHHH!" Morgan yelled back. "Caught! Red-handed! I'm guilty!" He threw down his newspaper in surrender. "Take me away! Shoot me! I did it! It was me! Take me— Hello!? *Hello? Are you there? Anybody? I'm— Hello? . . .*"

His father was asleep again.

Morgan collapsed on the floor in a crumpled heap and rolled over on his back. He closed his eyes and listened. Every so often the wind outside howled, and Morgan would get a whiff of fresh air that crept in the window he'd left open. The rain was puddling up in the gutters above and falling from the roof. It was a great sound, like a river, like an ocean, like a— Actually it *was* the ocean. Not falling from the roof, but coming from the TV.

Morgan cocked his head to the side and saw there was a fishing show on his father's sports channel. The screen was filled with blue—sky blue and ocean blue—Morgan couldn't tell where one ended and the other began. The sound of the sea tumbled into the living room. Every so often a streak of white screeched across the screen as a seagull flew past.

Morgan sat up to get a better look, but just as he did, a bright flash of lightning from outside whitened the room for a moment, and the TV went haywire. The volume leaped up and down, and the picture went in and out from blue to wiggly gray fuzz back to blue.

Suddenly Morgan smelled something weird and felt something funny under his feet. The floor was wet. Water was streaming in from one of the cracks in the ceiling.

Smoke was coming from the TV, filling the room. Morgan squirmed across the wet floor to get away from it.

"DAD!" Morgan screamed, sloshing toward the easy chair.

Morgan couldn't see his father through the smoke, but the reading lamp next to his chair was flashing on and off like a lighthouse.

Morgan tried to make his way toward it, but then another thundering crack of lightning rocked the building. Morgan staggered and fell backward into the easy chair, where his father no longer was.

"Dad!" he cried again. "Where are you? Mom! Somebody—"

The floor felt like it was moving now, like it was swelling and rolling under the chair. The ceiling creaked and crumbled. Rain and plaster showered down upon Morgan's head.

"Duck and cover," he thought. "Duck and cover."

The wind shrieked. The room trembled. Morgan screamed.

And then, just as suddenly as the storm had started, it stopped.

Everything was still. And quiet.

Morgan slowly lifted his head. The smoke cleared.

Above him now, where before was only a cracked plaster ceiling . . . was the deep, deep blue of a clear, quiet sky.

A seagull sailed silently through the living room.

Morgan's mouth dropped open. A clean,

fresh salt breeze startled his lungs, and he gasped. He couldn't move. He couldn't talk. He peered around the living room . . . and there wasn't one.

What there was instead was water. Everywhere. As far as he could see.

Morgan looked front and back and sideways. He leaned over the back of the chair. And gazed down into the deep. He couldn't see the bottom.

But he saw something.

Something moving.

A shape. A huge shape was coming toward him from the depths of his living-room floor. A great shadow of dark, growing larger and larger, charging toward the surface. The water stirred. Then it rippled and began to swirl. It churned and burbled white with foam, swelling upward, bulging. Suddenly a sharp spearlike object pierced through the water, and behind it streaked a brilliant flash of blue. The surface exploded in a burst of glittering water drops, spraying Morgan. The flash of blue flew upward, like a rocket, flying high above the surface, high above Morgan, a fluttering wisp of a white string trailing after it.

Morgan stared up in awe. The shape just hung there, where the ceiling used to be, hovering, nearly blocking out the sky.

It was a fish.

An unimaginably huge fish arching through the air of Morgan's living room.

A soaring mountain of blue.

It had a large scalloped fin fanning out from its back, like a glimmering sky-blue kite. Its monstrous head was a grayish blue, its belly silvery white; its nose tapered off into a long, sharp bill that ran out in front of itself like a javelin. From its mouth dangled a fishing line that disappeared into the water below. Its eyes were an impossible, deep blue-black, gray-yellow, and they seemed to be looking right at Morgan. The fish cocked its great head toward Morgan and *spoke* in a deep, rumbly voice that sounded like a low-batteried tape player.

"*Morgan,*" it said. "*Morgan.*"

Morgan couldn't speak. He couldn't *think*.

"*Morgan . . . COME . . .*" it sang in a low voice, and then began to fall.

Morgan watched as the great fish plummeted down and smacked into the water with a tremendous splash. The fishing line fluttered above for a moment, and Morgan tried to grab it, but the line shot through his hands, burning his fingers. The great fish raced away with lightning speed, straight out to where the walls of Morgan's living room used to be, straight toward the horizon where blue met blue. It zigged and zagged and thrashed its great head along the surface.

"It's caught," Morgan thought. "It's caught in the line." He tried to grab the line again, but it cut into his hand.

The great fish broke through the surface in a fury of thrashing and splashing. It smacked its tail and slapped its fins, rolling and twisting across the top of the water. It flailed its head back and forth and tried to throw a long, silvery hook that Morgan could now see embedded in its jaw.

Morgan wanted to help, but he didn't know what to do. He tried to gather up the line, but it tangled around his hands and the arms of the chair. In an instant the fish was high in the air again, soaring above Morgan's head.

Morgan's body tingled cool as the great eye of the fish looked at him once more.

"Morgan . . ." the voice said. *"COME."*

And then, with a powerful flick of its monstrous head—*WHACK!*—it snapped the line, spit the hook, and disappeared into the blue.

Morgan stared out where the fish used to be, where his *living* room used to be.

"This can't be happening," he thought. "I'm crazy. This is what crazy is."

Morgan tried to stay calm. He took a deep breath and closed his eyes.

He could taste the sea in the air. He could feel the gentle rocking of the living room. He could hear the ocean water slapping lazily against the sides of the easy chair, and his mother calling from the kitchen.

"Come on," she yelled, "both of you. Time for dinner!"

Morgan's eyes shot open. He looked around. He wasn't on the ocean. He was lying on the living-room floor in front of the TV.

"Someone turn off the TV," his mother said, coming into the room. "Time to eat."

Morgan jumped to his feet and spun around in a circle. He looked under the easy chair. He felt along the walls. He dropped to his knees and smelled the floor. He ran to the middle of the living room and started leaping up and down as hard as he could, testing the water—the *floor*—the floor that used to be the water.

His mother watched him with a worried look on her face.

"What are you doing?" his dad asked, as Morgan leaped circles around him.

Morgan pushed past his father, jumped into the easy chair, and searched over the sides. Then he stood in it and stared up at the ceiling, which was now only a ceiling.

"Get outta my chair!" his father said, making a sudden move toward him. "You're going to break it!"

Morgan dove over the side and tried to swim across the floor. It didn't work.

"Are you okay?" his mother asked. She knelt down and pressed a hand to his forehead. "You feel kind of warm. You—stop wiggling around so much—you slept half the day away."

"Slept," Morgan said. "Slept? I was sleeping? You sure?"

"Yes," his mother said. "You're your father's son, all right." She headed back toward the kitchen. "Stop jumping around and c'mon and eat before it gets cold."

"Dad! Dad, did the electricity go out before?"

"Electricity? What are you talking about?"

"Nothing."

Morgan shuffled backward down the hall toward the kitchen, keeping a suspicious eye on the living room. "That was *strange*," he thought, bumping into the open door of the bathroom—

"Ow."

The rest of the night Morgan couldn't think of anything except the great fish. It was like no dream he'd ever dreamed. All through dinner he kept seeing flashes of blue behind his eyes. Later that evening, when his father went back to sleep in the easy chair, Morgan positioned himself on the floor in exactly the same spot where he had been earlier. He stared at the ceiling, closed his eyes, and wished for the wind—for the dream, the hallucination, whatever it was—to come again. The image of the great fish haunted him. It came to him over and over—leaping out of the water, snapping the line, and splashing away.

"Leap, *snap*, splash!" Morgan said to himself. "Leap, *snap*, splash! . . . leap, *snap*—"

"Morgan, time for bed," his mother broke in. "It's getting late."

She came into the living room and gently woke his father up. As soon as she touched him, he sat bolt upright in his chair and cried out, *"I'm watching that!"* one last time before she guided him into their bedroom. She poked her head back out and said, "Go to sleep, Morgan. School tomorrow."

Morgan turned off the TV. It was still raining outside. He gently prodded the floor one more time, hoping it wouldn't be a floor, but it was. He looked at the ceiling. It was just a ceiling.

"My hands!" he thought, remembering how the fishing line had cut his hands.

He looked at them. Nothing. They were the same. Everything was the same . . . everything except for the shiny silvery hook lying beneath the TV.

A sparkle of wonder tingled down Morgan's back.

He closed his eyes and opened them again. It was still there.

Slowly he reached under the TV, waiting for the hook to disappear, but it didn't. He touched it with the tip of his finger, he poked it, he scooted it across the floor a little. He picked it up and turned it over in his hands. It was cold and hard. He held it up before his eyes and twisted it from side to side. He looked at himself and the hook, reflected in the darkened screen of the TV, and both were gleaming.

"It's real," he whispered softly, "it's real." And slowly he closed his fingers around the hook.

The rain still rained, the wind knocked gently against the kitchen window that he had never closed, and for a moment, Morgan thought—no, Morgan *knew*—he could smell the sea.

On this rainy Sunday-like-any-other-Sunday, something in Morgan changed.

CHAPTER THREE

Mrs. McSwiggen knocked, not so gently, on the back of Morgan's head to wake him up during math class. That was her real name. She stood about four foot six and had flabby pouches of skin, right above both her elbows, that flapped back and forth whenever she walked, or waddled. She was very heavy for her size. No, she was fat. She was just plain fat. And you can't afford to be fat when you're four foot six.

"Knock, knock, knock. Anybody home?" Mrs. McSwiggen asked, rapping on Morgan's head, still thinking he was sleeping. He wasn't. His head was down and his eyes were shut, but his mind was racing with wild thoughts about what had happened the day before— the ocean, the great fish, the *hook*—it was all too weird and wonderful. The memory of it was as real as any other memory he'd ever had. And the hook was definitely real. He had it right in his front pocket—

"*HELLO?*" Mrs. McSwiggen crooned, leaning into Morgan's ear.

Morgan squeezed his eyes shut tighter and tried to make the dream come again, tried to make math class blow away just the way his living room had done on Sunday. It didn't. Morgan looked up.

"Well, good morning! So nice of you to join us today."

The class snickered.

"Somebody think this is funny?!" Mrs. McSwiggen warned. "Well?" The room fell silent, and she resumed her interrogation of Morgan. "So, were you having a nice dream? Would you like to share it with the class?"

Morgan tried to stifle a yawn but couldn't.

"Am I boring you, Morgan?"

"Yes, you are, you blimpy old witch!" he wanted to say but didn't. "No," he said instead.

"Good. Then maybe you would like to finish the equation that's up on the blackboard."

There was a moment of silence in the room.

Morgan looked up from his desk. There it

was. *Math.* Lots of it. Everywhere Morgan looked. Fractions and fractions of math!! He felt a little dizzy.

"Yes, why don't you?" Mrs. McSwiggen said in a near whisper, handing him the chalk. Her thumb was twitching. "Why don't you just do that for us, Mr. *I-can-sleep-during-math* man."

With great effort Morgan extricated himself from behind his desk. Head bowed, he trudged up the aisle like a condemned man.

"Yes, you just show us how it's done, Mr. *I'm-so-good-at-this-I-don't-need-to-pay-attention* man."

Finally, he made it to the front of the class. He stood there, staring down at the laces in his red-and-white sneakers.

"You're not going to find the answers on the floor, now, are you, Mr. *Sleepy-student-head.*"

"*Sleepy-student-head?*" Morgan mumbled under his breath.

"I'm sorry, did you say something?" Mrs. McSwiggen hissed from the back of the room. "If you did, then say it loud enough so the whole class can hear."

"No. I didn't—"

"What?! I can't hear you!"

"I didn't say anything!"

"I didn't think so. Stop wasting time. You're not going anywhere till you finish."

The class *oooh*ed.

"And neither is anyone else!" she added.

There was no escaping. The room was soundless. Morgan lifted his head and stared up at the dreaded blackboard.

"It's green," he thought. "The board is green."

"Anytime, young man."

"Why do they call it a blackboard when it's green?"

"Begin!"

Slowly, Morgan raised the chalk. His hand was sweating and the chalk was sticking to his fingers. With his other hand he fished around in his front pocket until he felt the cold steel of the great silvery hook he had taken with him. It was still there.

"Okay, just stay calm," he coached himself. "Okay, *one third* . . ."

He never finished writing the three in *one third*. He should have stopped with the second half loop in the number three, but instead he continued on and started to make what looked like the number eight, but that continued too. The loops just kept . . . looping! Morgan tried to stop it—to get the loops under control and make the three—but he couldn't. He couldn't stop his hand. The little loops turned into bigger loops, and pretty soon he was making sweeping circles all across the board, then huge sort of *W*'s that started to look like waves. They were *waves*! Morgan, or his hand, or the chalk, or something, was drawing waves! All over Mrs. McSwiggen's math! Then he started to draw birds. Beautiful seabirds, laughing gulls and other birds he had never even seen before, flying through clouds of algebra. And *fish*, lots of fish! Fish he had had no idea even existed. And then he started to draw the *great fish*, right smack in the middle of the crowded sea-green board. It was bigger than all the other fish put together. He drew the top fin like a huge blue billowy sail, and then the bill, the long swordlike bill, sharp . . . and the eyes . . . the great eyes, steel-blue eyes that—

Mrs. McSwiggen dug her little nails into Morgan's wrist.

"You think you're funny, mister?" she

cackled. "Well, we'll see how funny it is when you wash every blackboard in this school!"

Morgan looked down at the purple crescents indented in his wrist.

"Every single one!" she continued.

When Morgan looked up at the board again, at all the beautiful drawings, his mouth opened slightly. He couldn't believe what he saw.

There were no birds, no waves, no great fish. There was only a mess of scribbled lines and crossed-out math problems.

The class was amused.

"Settle down. Settle down! Unless you'd like to join him?" Mrs. McSwiggen threatened. Then she turned back to Morgan. "We'll see how funny your parents think it is."

Right then Morgan wished she were a mackerel. He didn't even know what a mackerel was, but he knew it was something a great fish could eat, and if he were a great fish, that's exactly what he'd do, *eat her*! A chubby, flabby, waddling, green mackerel—*CHOMP!* No more McSwiggen—*CHOMP!* No more math!

But instead of eating his teacher, Morgan cleaned thirty-two greenboards that afternoon.

CHAPTER FOUR

MORGAN'S MOTHER WAS CLEANING the china when he got home from school. Well, they didn't actually have china, just plates and better plates that they *called* china, and she was cleaning them. She liked to clean things when she was mad: silverware, lamps, windows, tile floors, rugs, ceilings, and Morgan.

"Go take a bath," she said.

Morgan knew he was in trouble whenever his mother said that. Other kids got sent to their rooms, Morgan to the tub.

He went into the bathroom and turned on the faucet. His mother swung open the door and stuck her head in. "I don't know what you think you're up to lately," she cried. "But whatever it is, cut it out! I've got to go down to school and talk to Mrs. McSwiggen tomorrow. You want me to tell your father that? Hm? Do you?"

"No," Morgan said. "I . . . it's just . . . it was

green and . . . it . . . the . . . *math*—"

"I don't want to hear any excuses! You behave in school, or I'm going to tell your father!" she said, and slammed the door.

Morgan got undressed and stepped into the tub.

"That's weird," he thought. "The water's cold."

The water wasn't just cold like cold from sitting around too long, but cold like *ice* cold.

What was weirder was it felt great. Morgan sat in the tub. He leaned back and let himself slide under the water. He stayed there with his eyes open, holding his breath. He stared at the ceiling for a long time.

"I wonder what the sky looks like to a fish," he wondered underwater.

After a while Morgan began to turn a little blue. Not blue like the great fish was blue, but blue like he hadn't breathed in a long time blue. He flung his head and body up out of the water and shook furiously from side to side, splattering water all over the bathroom. He took a deep breath and dove back under.

"It's quiet down here," he thought.

He tapped his fingers on the bottom of the

tub. He tapped again. The lightest tap made sounds that echoed through his whole body. He looked at his hands. He could see every line in his palm, and every swirl on his fingertips, like they were under a microscope. Everything was clearer under water. Things were bigger, and sharper. He could even—

"GASP!!" (He had forgotten to breathe.)

Morgan took another deep breath and dove under again. He tried to turn around and swim to the other end, but there wasn't enough room. He kept knocking his head into the sides of the tub.

"Stuck," he said to himself. "Tubbed in."

He thought of the great fish and how it probably never whacked its head into the sides of bathtubs—it wouldn't even be able to *fit* in one. He remembered how it had leaped through the air, and he imagined what it must feel like to leap like that, to fly, to sail through the—

Morgan leaped out of the water.

As far as he could.

Over and over again.

He kept both hands behind his back, like a dorsal fin, and flailed his body and head from side to side each time he broke the surface.

"I need more space," he thought, mid leap. "I can't leap in a tub. I need more—"

That was when his mother walked in.

"Well, see, I was in the ocean, right?" Morgan tried to explain. "And, and I was a fish, a *great* fish, and—"

His mother was not interested in this explanation.

Morgan was grounded for two weeks.

CHAPTER FIVE

"**W**ELL, I HOPE you understand how this kind of behavior cannot be tolerated. It upsets the entire . . . blah, blah, blah . . ." barked Mrs. McSwiggen like a trained seal. Morgan's mother sat next to him, squeezing his hand.

". . . and if he can't pay attention in class, then he . . ." bark, bark.

His mother was quiet—too quiet. Each time Morgan squirmed in his chair, she squeezed his hand a little harder until he stopped. They both sat staring straight ahead, pretending they were listening.

". . . especially in MATH class, which is one of the most important fundamentals of all . . ." woof, woof, WOOF!

His mother nodded in agreement and stood up quickly, with Morgan dangling along her side. She nodded again to Mrs. McSwiggen and quickly left the room with Morgan in tow.

"You think I've got nothing better to do after work than run all the way across town to talk to your teachers?" she said, hustling Morgan down the steps of the school. "Do you?"

Morgan remained silent.

"I've got enough to do, okay? I don't need trouble from you now."

They passed the school playground, where some kids were playing basketball.

"Time out!" one of the boys yelled when he saw Morgan. Both teams stopped playing and ran over to the story-high chain-link fence.

Morgan tried to pry his fingers out from his mother's grasp, but she held on even tighter.

"Hey, momma's boy!" they yelled, rattling the fence and hooting. "Look who's walking home with his momma! Woo-hoo!"

Morgan covered his face like criminals on TV who don't want to be seen by the camera. The playground laughed louder. His mother was unmoved.

She walked Morgan the rest of the way home in silence.

When they turned the corner of their

block, a low rumble of thunder rolled across the gray sky.

"Perfect," his mother growled, glancing up. "Just perfect."

She covered her head with her purse and walked faster. Morgan jogged alongside, trying to keep up.

"In," she said, ushering him up the steps to their building. "In."

"Can I sit outside?" Morgan asked as she ducked inside the doorway.

"You're grounded, mister. Remember? You're not going anywhere."

"I never go anywhere anyway," Morgan said, lingering on the steps. "I'll stay on the stoop."

"It's going to rain again."

"Please?"

"Don't argue with me now, Morgan, okay? I've got to clean and get dinner ready or your father'll go through the roof."

"I'll be out of your way out here. I won't bother you."

His mother looked up at the sky and then at Morgan. She had her "overwhelmed" look on her face, which was how she looked most of the time, like she was always doing a hundred things at once but never had time enough to do any of them.

"Oh for— Go—go get a jacket," she said distractedly.

Morgan ran up the stoop, squeezing past his mother, and dashed down the long dark hallway of their building.

"And if it starts to rain, you get inside. That's all I need is for you to get sick."

"Okay!"

"And the *third* step," she added, still negotiating. "You don't go past the third step!"

"I know," Morgan called back.

The magical third step down.

Whenever Morgan got grounded—which happened kind of a lot—there were different degrees of just how grounded he actually *was*. The worst, of course, was having to stay in his room, but sometimes, for lesser offenses, he'd be allowed to sit outside on the stoop, but he could never go past the third step.

As soon as he was out of his mother's sight, Morgan bounded up the three flights of stairs to their apartment. He was excited and *hoping* it would rain. He had never liked the rain

before, but for some reason now he loved it—
the feel of it, the smell, even the sound was
exciting to him. He threw on his goofy yellow
rain slicker that reminded him of cartoon
ducks, rifled through the junk drawer and
grabbed some black electrical tape, and ran
back out in the hall. He leaped down the stairs,
clearing three to four steps with each jump,
saying to himself, *"Leap, snap, splash. . . . Leap,
snap, splash. . . ."*

He met his mother halfway down.

"And no TV," she reminded Morgan as he
leaped past her. "Two weeks."

"Yup," he called back, as he slipped on the
last step and crashed into the wall on the land-
ing.

"Morgan!" his mother yelled.

"I'm all right," he said quickly, more embarrassed than bruised. "I'm fine."

"You're going to break your neck one of
these days. Slow down."

"I'm fine," Morgan assured her, ready to run.

"Walk."

"I—"

"WALK."

Morgan walked down the last flight of

steps. His mother watched him the whole way.

It was drizzling now. The streets were empty. Morgan stood in the entryway and took out the electrical tape. He snaked his hand under his yellow slicker, dug into his pockets, and took out the great silvery hook. He pulled his pocket inside out along with it. The hook was snagged in his pants again. The same thing had happened at school a few times. That was why he had the electrical tape.

Morgan walked down to the third step. He sat down and placed the hook on the yellow slicker stretched tight across his knees. He pulled off a length of black electrical tape and wrapped it around the end of the hook, just enough to cover the barbed end so it wouldn't snag his pants anymore. Then he closed both hands over it and looked out over the abandoned block.

It was raining harder now, but Morgan didn't mind. He pulled up his hood and listened to the rain *pop-pop-pop* on his head. He stared across the street at the rows of buildings all exactly like the one that he lived in. He could have been looking in a mirror, he thought, only he wasn't in the reflection.

Morgan opened his hands and looked down at the hook. The tape wrapped on the end of it looked like a wad of black bait for some fantastical sea creature. He twirled the hook between his fingers and remembered how the great fish had thrashed and splashed and finally snapped the line.

"I would do that," he daydreamed. "If I were a great fish, I would do that."

"Morgan!" his mother called down from the window three floors above. "It's raining. Get in here."

"C'mon, Mom!" Morgan pleaded upward.

"You're going to catch pneumonia," she said. "In."

"All right. In a minute."

His mother slammed the window shut.

Morgan held the hook up and looked at it against the smoggy sky. He thought of the great fish swimming through the dreariness above, high above the rooftops of the city, leaping through the dark clouds in lightning-bright flashes of blue.

He let the hook drop into his slickered lap. Rainwater puddled up and ran over it. Morgan followed the water as it zigzagged down the folds of his slicker, like little rivers hurrying down creased rubber valleys. The water glided over him, down the folds of his slicker, under and around his shoes, down the third step, cascading beyond to the forbidden steps far below—the seventh step, the eighth, the ninth, onto the sneakers of the man who—

Morgan's head shot up. There was a man standing at the bottom of the stoop, staring up at him.

Morgan quickly scooted up the stoop, crablike, and stopped when his back hit the door of the building. The hook fell from his lap and clinkled down the stoop, coming to rest on the last step, right in front of the stranger.

"What—what do you want?" Morgan asked, trying not to sound frightened.

The man just stood there.

He was wearing an overcoat, darkened wet by the rain, a baseball cap, and sunglasses. He was hunched over, and his hands were in his coat pockets.

"I'll call the cops!" Morgan threatened, his back to the door.

The man didn't move. Rain dripped off the bill of his baseball cap. He stared at Morgan.

Morgan reached behind and opened the door to the building. He backed into the doorway, keeping an eye on the man.

"*Morgan* . . ." the man said in a low, rumbly voice.

Morgan's body goose-bumped cold.

It was the same voice.

The same voice that he had heard in his dream . . . the voice of the great fish.

It seemed to echo in Morgan's head.

"How . . . how do you know my name?" Morgan asked.

The man said nothing.

"What do you want?" Morgan demanded.

Again the man said nothing. He took his hands out of his pockets, and Morgan saw that he was wearing gloves. The man took off his hat. Rain pattered off his bald head.

Morgan scrunched his eyes in the rain to see the man better. He was old. Not *old* old, but old.

The man smiled a slight little smile at Morgan and shook his head from side to side to shake the water from his face. He took off his sunglasses. His eyes were huge and round.

And they were *blue*.

Not everyday blue, but brilliant ice-blue-streaks-with-huge-black-pupils-floating-in-them blue.

THEY WERE EYES JUST LIKE THE GREAT FISH'S!

Morgan let out a little cry and rushed into the building, slamming the door behind him. He was just about to run up the stairs when—

"*Morgan . . .*"

The voice called again. The word filled the hallway, long and low, almost humming. It buzzed through Morgan, like his whole body was one big funny bone that had just been banged.

"*Morgan . . . come. . . .*"

Morgan opened the door. Slowly.

The man was still there, still smiling a little half smile.

"*Morgan,*" the man said, and Morgan noticed something.

The man's mouth did not move when he spoke.

"*Don't be scared.*"

Again the words seemed to buzz through Morgan, as if he were hearing with his body, not his ears. But it didn't scare Morgan. It calmed him. Morgan opened the door all the way and walked outside.

He was not afraid.

Morgan stood at the top of the stoop and looked down at the old man on the sidewalk. The old man looked up at Morgan. His eyes were way too big for his face, Morgan thought, and his feet too large for his legs.

The old man put his sunglasses back on.

"What you're thinking, Morgan," the man said, nodding his head softly. *"Believe it."*

"Believe what?" Morgan asked. "What . . . what are you talking about? Who are you?"

The old man put his hat back on and tugged it down low on his forehead.

"Are you . . . ?" Morgan struggled to ask the man. "Do you have something to do with—"

"MORGAN!" his mother yelled from the window above. "NOW!"

"In a second!" Morgan yelled instinctively, turning and looking up at the slamming window.

Morgan heard the clink of metal on the stoop.

He spun back around.

The man was gone, vanished, dissolved, nowhere.

The silvery hook was on the third step.

Morgan grabbed the hook and scurried down the stoop. He looked up and down the block—nothing. He ran into the middle of the street to get a better look—nothing. He looked back at his building and saw his mother staring out the front window at him.

"Aw, *man!*" he moaned out loud, nailed, remembering he'd left the stoop.

His mother gave him a You're-in-trouble-now-mister look, and waved him inside.

Morgan started back in and was just about to open the door of the building when he heard—*felt*—the voice again.

"Believe it."

CHAPTER SIX

MORGAN WAS GROUNDED for *another* week for leaving the stoop.

He didn't tell his mother or father about the old man. "I'd get in enough trouble for talking to a stranger," Morgan thought, "never mind talking to some mutant alien kind of fish guy. They'd think I was crazy anyway. Maybe I am."

"I'm going to the library after school today, Mom," he told his mother the next morning.

"Oh, no you're not, mister," she said immediately. "You forget you're grounded?"

"I have to. It's for a science project."

"Oh," she said, considering this. "Well, you come *right* home after that. You understand me?"

"Okay."

Morgan wanted to find a picture of the fish he had seen—or dreamed, or felt, or whatever. He wanted to *see* it.

After school he stopped off at the public library and went to the magazine racks. He gathered up all of the fishing magazines he could find: *Sports Afield, American Outdoorsman, The Bassmaster, Saltwater Fishing, Field & Stream*—anything to do with fish.

He lugged them back to an empty table in the far corner of the library, away from everyone else, and spread them about before him. Everywhere he looked there were fish leaping across the covers of the magazines. He didn't know where to begin. He didn't have to. There, right in front of him, on the cover of *Saltwater Fishing*, was a great glossy color photo of the great fish.

The same exact one.

Or at least it looked exactly the same.

Morgan could barely contain his excitement, but he did. He snatched up the magazine and read the title of the article.

"'Sailfishing.'"

He liked the word.

"'Sailfishing,'" he continued to read. "'The Ultimate Guide to Blue Marlin—'"

"Marlin!" Morgan exclaimed out loud, reading the word again. "Marlin!" A head or two turned in his direction. He didn't care. "That's it. My fish. It's a *marlin. A blue marlin.*"

The picture was beautiful. Just as he remembered the great fish. He ran his fingers over the cover and traced its outline. It was all there: the huge fin like a scalloped sky-blue kite, the great spearlike nose, the eyes—the eyes were the same too, just like his fish's—just like the old man's!

His feet tingled when he had the thought.

Morgan wanted to smell the ocean again. He wanted to *touch* the marlin, to *be* the marlin. He wanted to *steal* the magazine.

"A marlin shouldn't be in a library," he rationalized. "Or in a tub!"

But then he thought that if he were caught stealing, he'd probably get grounded for the rest of his life. So instead of stealing the magazine, Morgan decided to just take the picture of the marlin.

He turned his back to the checkout desk and carefully tore off the front cover, hiding the sounds of the ripping under a fake coughing fit.

"*Cough*"—rip ... "*cough*"—rip ... "*cough*"— RIP!

He folded it up and slipped it into the inside pocket of his jacket. He quickly culled through the other magazines and found another article on marlins in *American Outdoorsman*. He had to be getting home soon, so Morgan grabbed the *American Outdoorsman* magazine and left the others on the table, hiding the coverless *Saltwater Fishing* under a *Field & Stream*. He didn't want to call attention to himself, so he thought he should check something else out along with the magazine. He figured it should be something that made him look studious.

"Something fat," he decided. "A fat book."

He pulled down *Beginning Math and Fundamentals of Algebra* from the book stacks, headed to the front desk, and checked it out along with the magazine.

Oh so casually, he said, "Thank you," to the librarian and strolled out the doors, waiting for every alarm in the building to go off and security guards to come rushing over and tackle him and drag him away kicking and screaming to the police station for cover stealing.

They didn't.

As soon as he got outside the doors, he dumped the math book in the night deposit slot and ran all the way home. When he got there, he locked himself in his room, carefully unfolded the picture of the marlin that was in his pocket, and tacked it up on the wall next to his bed.

It was wonderful.

Then he took out the *American Outdoorsman* magazine. The article had a slew of other pictures of blue marlins. He cut them all out and tacked them up on the wall alongside the *great* marlin and read the article.

He read it again.

And again.

It was filled with all kinds of information about marlins: how big they get, where they live, how high they can leap, how fast they are. But the thing that struck Morgan most was a story near the end of the article. It was about some guys who had caught a marlin alive so they could tame it and teach it to do tricks like a dolphin—jump through hoops and pop balloons with its pointy bill. So the guys caught their marlin and brought it back and put it in a special pool they'd set up. The marlin was a little dazed at first. It tried to leap, but the water was too shallow for it to get a running start, so it could only do these feeble little hops that looked like it was doing a butterfly stroke or something. For more than four hours it tried to leap. Then it began to swim in small circles, bumping into the walls sometimes and smacking them with its tail. For two *more* hours it did this. Then, suddenly, it wheeled toward the center of the pool, skimmed across the surface to the far end, darted to one side, and began swimming the length of the pool as fast as it could. It reversed directions, cut across on diagonals, and tried to leap—faster and faster each time, heading toward one wall, then turning around and heading toward another, then hugging the sides and circling with lightning speed around and around the pool, over and over again—until it suddenly stopped.

Completely.

It just stopped perfectly still . . . eased itself to the center of the pool and just . . . hung there . . . a few feet below the surface . . . suspended for a moment . . . and then its great marlin body slowly and gracefully turned itself belly up . . . and floated to the surface.

It was dead.

Untamed and dead.

"Morgan! Dinner!" his mom called from the kitchen. "Morgan!?"

"Right there, Mom!" he promised as he stashed the magazine under his bed. Something in Morgan's body tingled again, like when he had first seen the great marlin.

"Morgan, now!" his mother warned.

"Coming!"

Morgan slammed the door to his room and headed toward the kitchen. "Hi, Dad," he said as he sat down at the table, his head still swimming with marlin thoughts.

"Mm," his dad said, buried behind a newspaper.

"Hi, Dad," Morgan said again.

His father lowered his paper a few inches. "What?" he asked, annoyed.

"Hi."

"Oh," he said suspiciously. "Hi."

"Leave your father alone," his mom cautioned Morgan. She put the food on the table.

"What's this?" Morgan asked painfully as he looked at his plate.

"What do you mean, what's this? It's food," his mother answered. "Spaghetti and salad. You like spaghetti."

"Yeah, but you know I don't like the salad part," Morgan said carefully.

"Eat," mumbled the newspaper.

"Just try it. How do you know if you never try it?"

Morgan's mother always put all kinds of things in his salad, things nobody should ever have to eat: black olives, hot peppers, celery sticks, anchovies—

"Anchovies?" Morgan thought.

The strangest feeling came over him. He wanted to try the anchovies. He hated anchovies, but he suddenly had an uncontrollable urge to grab a mess of them and gobble them down.

And he did.

Just as his father was going for a forkful, Morgan leaped in and snatched them up with one stab—every last one of them—and gulped them down . . . SHLURRP!! Gone.

"Mmm . . ." he thought. "Salt. Really salty and . . . mushy. Mush, mush, mush, mmm!!"

His father was still frozen in the same position. He and his fork were hovering above the spot where the anchovies used to be. He stared at Morgan for a moment and then calmly changed the direction that his fork was going and speared an olive. He said nothing . . . just leaned back in his chair and gave his mother the *look*. The You'd-better-do-something-or-I-will look.

"Since when do you like anchovies?" Mom asked.

"Are there any more?" he asked back.

His mother looked at him. Then she looked at his father. Then she went to get another can of anchovies. His father intercepted her on her way back to the table and took a helping before Morgan could get to them. Morgan took the rest and—

SHLUUURRP!!

Mom was still staring at him. She looked a little puzzled. "I'll buy more next time," she whispered to his father, putting a bowl of spaghetti in front of him.

"Mm," he said, stabbing a nest of it and slopping it onto his plate.

His father fork twirled his spaghetti with one hand and read his paper with the other. Mom ate like a bird, occasionally glancing over at his father, then back down to her plate. Morgan craved more anchovies.

There was nothing but the rustle of newspaper and clink of forks for a long time.

"I want to be a marlin!!" Morgan suddenly blurted out.

Silence from the dinner table.

His father didn't look up from his plate, just stared at it and stopped chewing. His mother paused, fork in hand, and also stopped chewing for a moment. Then they both went back to eating as if nothing had been said.

"I want to be a marlin!!" Morgan said again.

His father grumbled from somewhere in his plate and spoke.

"Yeah, and I want to be six foot two."

His father was about five foot three. Whenever anybody wanted something they couldn't have, this was his stock reply.

His mother was a little more understanding.

"Sure, honey. You can be anything you want. Just study hard. Now eat."

"Well . . . I just wanted to let you know," he added.

"Mm" from both of them.

That night the fever started.

CHAPTER SEVEN

MORGAN LAY AWAKE in bed. He was sweaty and hot. His mind raced with thoughts of the marlin and of the marlin man he had seen on the stoop.

"If he's what I think he is, what's he doing in the city?" he thought. "What was he doing talking to me!? Why isn't he out in the ocean, in the open sea, wandering the world?"

He kicked the covers off.

"Well, he wasn't *really* a marlin . . . but he had those eyes, and the same voice. No mistaking that."

He sat up in his bed and picked up the silvery hook, which was on the table next to his bed.

"Who wouldn't be a marlin if they could?"

A drop of sweat rolled down onto Morgan's lips, and he lapped it up. It tasted salty. There was still a little corner of his blanket covering his feet. He kicked at it furiously until it was nowhere near him. He didn't want anything touching him. He rolled onto his side, and the bed sheet came with him, stuck to his arms and legs. His whole body was sweating.

Something was wrong.

He pulled his knees up under his chin and stared at the marlin pictures hanging on the wall. He was starting to feel a little dizzy. He began rocking very gently from side to side, but that just made him feel worse. He got out of the bed and tore off his T-shirt and underwear. They were suffocating him. He wanted them off his body. He wanted nothing touching his skin. He didn't even want the floor to touch his feet. He wanted to be floating somewhere. Somewhere cool and wet.

He opened the window in his room and stuck his head out. He watched his sweat drip-drop down three floors to the pavement below. He looked up at the sky, and there wasn't one, just another building bigger than his.

He was having trouble breathing. His throat was dry. Inside his chest was dry. It felt like he was a sponge that was shriveling up, getting smaller and tighter.

Slowly . . . slowly, walking like an old man, he made his way to the bedroom door. He opened it and headed toward the bathroom with only one thought on his mind:

"Water."

It was all he could think of. A craving like nothing before in his life overtook him. Walking down the hall took an eternity. When he arrived at the bathroom, he mummied straight into the tub.

He reached down and twisted open the cold water. It burst out with a splash.

"OH! OH! YES!"

The cold water poured over his feet and started to wrap around his ankles.

"OH! Oh, yes, yes!"

He stood there for a short while. A cool sensation began in his toes and started making its way up his body. Morgan sat down in the tub.

"AHHHH! Oh! OH! Thank you, yes, thank you, water, thank you."

He let the water run till it tickled his elbows, then laid himself back, carefully, and slunk under the water as far as he could.

"Ohhhh, yesssss . . . I can breathe again. I can breathe, I . . . ahhhh . . ."

Morgan lay there, without moving, for a long time. He thought of the blue water he had seen on the TV and of the smell of the ocean, of salt hanging in the air and waves crashing upon the shore, of the screech of gulls overhead, of blue-green waters beyond imagination.

And he dreamed of being a marlin.

He would be the fastest of all the marlins—of all marlinhood!—blinding men with his speed, scorching the surface of the ocean as he ran circles around anyone who was foolish enough to try to catch him. He imagined himself sounding to the depths of the ocean, brushing the sandy bottom with his tail and, without stopping, heading up again toward the surface—gathering speed—the shimmering white circle of the sun growing larger and larger as he neared the surface—faster now!—the sound of water rushing past his ears!—almost to the top!—another thrust of his great marlin tail and—

"Marlins can't live in bathtubs," he thought, and sank back a little lower under the water.

"What on earth do you think you're doing?" his mother asked wearily as she leaned against the bathroom doorway, pink robed and slippered. Morgan sat up slowly.

"Taking a bath?" he suggested.

"It's two o'clock in the morning! You get yourself—"

"I don't feel good, Mom."

Her voice softened in an instant.

"What's the matter?" she asked.

"I was just hot, Mom, really hot. I couldn't sleep, I—"

She grabbed his head and pulled it toward her, pressing his forehead against her cheek. They were both very still for a moment, like she was listening for something very important and hard to hear.

"You've got a fever," she diagnosed.

"I was just hot. I feel a lot better now."

"Shhh . . . just sit still. Hand me that."

Morgan handed her the washcloth, and his mother sponged the cool water down the back of his neck. She was sitting on the edge of the tub, fuzzy sleeves rolled up, doing what moms do best, untiringly.

"Feeling better?" she asked.

"Mm-hmm."

"Okay, let's try and get us back to bed. Come on now."

His mother helped him out of the tub and hugged him into his favorite towel, gently patting him down. They walked down the hallway together, trying not to wake up his father.

Morgan threw a pair of shorts on and climbed into bed as his mother billowed a fresh white cotton sheet over him. While it was still settling down, she pulled up a chair by the bed. They were both very quiet for a long time.

"Those are pretty," she said, finally, nodding to the marlin pictures on the wall.

"They're marlins."

"Marlins, huh?"

"Yup. Marlins. Blue marlins."

"Blue? . . . Pretty."

"That's what I want to be. Like I said at dinner."

His mother was silent.

"A marlin," Morgan said again.

"That's a fish, honey."

"I know."

"Go to sleep now."

"Look how high that one's jumping! Must be ten feet! And that one . . . how blue he is . . . and the stripes on him—"

"Shhh, shh . . . go to sleep, honey."

"They swim all over the world. Anywhere they want. And nobody can catch them. Hardly ever. And if they are caught, they die. They just die. 'Cause they have to swim. They have to keep swimming."

"Mm-hmm," his mother hummed reassuringly.

"And that one there!? See him? No, that guy over there . . . yeah, him! He's an old one. A really old one. Isn't he huge? And that one! See! He looks like he's flying, doesn't he!?"

Morgan's mother looked down at him. She had a funny little smile on her face.

"Yes he does," she said softly just before Morgan fell asleep. "He looks like he's flying."

CHAPTER EIGHT

THE NEXT DAY Morgan didn't have to go to school.

"Anchovies!" Morgan's mother yelled from the kitchen. "I bet it was those stupid anchovies. You ate half a can!"

Morgan was envisioning a great day home from school. No Mrs. McSwiggen, and no homework. He reached under his bed and grabbed the *American Outdoorsman* magazine from the library. He was just settling down to page through it when the fever struck again.

It was incredible how quickly it overtook him. His face flashed red and his throat closed up. He could hardly breathe. He tried to call for his mother, but he couldn't. His voice sounded all gargly and strange, like cats when they choke on hairballs. He tried desperately to get more air into his lungs. He leaned forward, arms outstretched, gulping for air, looking like some bedridden guppy.

"You've never eaten an anchovy in your—" his mother started to say as she came back into the room. She stopped when she saw Morgan. Then she ran to him, felt his head, and rushed out of the room. She hurried back in with wet towels, laid them across his chest and head, and then got on the phone to Mrs. Pasalaqua.

Mrs. Pasalaqua was a widow who lived right below them with a green parakeet named Uncle Pete. She'd been alone ever since Morgan could remember. She and his mother would often have coffee together or something a little stronger depending on what time of day it was. Mrs. Pasalaqua was always called in emergencies. If someone was sick and you didn't know what to do, you called Mrs. Pasalaqua. She was sort of the building's resident physician. She could do anything, from piercing ears with just an ice cube and a sewing needle to reading your future in the bottom of a teacup. You never called a doctor without first consulting with Mrs. Pasalaqua.

Morgan heard her coming in the front door. "Where'sa he?" she asked very professionally. His mother showed her into Morgan's room. Mrs. Pasalaqua eyed him from the doorway, making her initial observation. She strode in and placed the back of her hand against his neck, his forehead, and then his stomach.

"Maybe you get some ice," she said, not meaning *maybe* at all. Mrs. Pasalaqua had come over on the boat, and the little English she spoke was thick as olive oil.

"Maybe you go fast," she added. "Two, three bags."

His mother grabbed her purse and headed out to the deli on the corner.

"Whaddyou make trouble here for? You make Momma worry?" Mrs. Pasalaqua teased, continuing to feel and poke different parts of Morgan's body.

"Now, you go nowhere. I be righta back."

Morgan heard her rummaging around in the kitchen: the clink of glass, a cupboard opening. She came back to the room with a glass of something for him to drink, sat down, and drank it herself.

"You make-a me hot I just look at you."

His mother came back with two bags of ice. Mrs. Pasalaqua finished her drink and went to meet her. Morgan watched them huddle in the kitchen for a moment. Then they both came back and helped him to the bathroom and out of his underwear. Into the tub went the two bags of ice, a little water, and Morgan.

"AHHHH!" Morgan breathed in relief.

The ice felt good. Both ladies sat on the edge of the tub and sponged the cold water down his back and over his shoulders and arms. Morgan was too dazed to be embarrassed. His temperature wouldn't go down.

"So hot isa no good," Mrs. Pasalaqua warned. I think we call nine one one."

"No! I feel a lot better already. Really," Morgan gargled.

"Whata you say?"

"What's wrong with your voice, Morgan?" his mother asked.

"Nothing. Just a little dry," Morgan said with a shrug, but it came out: "Uggin. Ush uh liggle eye."

"What?" they both said.

"Ai oat ish uh liggle eye." *(My throat is a little dry.)*

Mrs. Pasalaqua and Mom looked at each other for a short moment.

"I think we get him backa to bed," Mrs.

Pasalaqua prescribed. "We keep hima wet, yes?"

They wrapped a wet towel around Morgan and helped him back to his room.

"You need me more, stompa the floor. I come," Mrs. Pasalaqua said on her way out.

Mom saw her to the door.

In bed Morgan felt hot again. He tried focusing on the great marlin up on his wall. He imagined himself in the picture and tried to move it with his thoughts. He tried to make the marlin's fins move by wiggling his hands, and then the tail by flip-flapping his feet. He tried them separately and then both at once. Nothing happened. Then he tried moving his head. Morgan wanted the great marlin to slap his head in the water so he could feel the cool splash of the sea. He flung his head from side to side, all the while keeping one eye on the marlin. Nothing happened except that his father appeared in the doorway, home from work for the day. He was still in his business clothes: suit-and-tied, briefcased, trussed up, and weighted down.

"What's going on?" he asked.

"Morgan's been sick all day," his mom answered. "Fever."

"Hmm." He paused a moment. Then he was gone again. Nothing came in the way of his father changing his clothes after coming home from work. It was always the first thing he did.

"Does it hurt when you talk?" Mom asked.

Morgan nodded yes.

"I'm gonna fix some supper. Want some?"

He shook his head no.

"Okay. Call if you need anything . . . or . . . throw something."

His mother kissed him and then went to nurse the other male in the house. Morgan went back to staring at the marlin on the wall.

"Do you dream?" he asked the picture. "Were you always a marlin?" And then suddenly a crazy thought popped out. "Am I one of you?"

He closed his eyes and tried to imagine what it would be like to turn into a fish.

"It would feel exactly like I feel right now!" Morgan thought. "It would . . . I mean . . . I'd be a fish out of water, so . . . I'd be thirsty, right?! And . . . drying out, and . . . I'd need . . . lots of fluids!"

Morgan sat up and shook himself all over.

"What a stupid thought," he thought. "People don't just become marlins. You're either born one or you're not. You don't get to choose your species."

Then he remembered the old man.

"Well," he thought, "it was raining and I couldn't really see that well. Maybe his eyes were just, sort of, done with makeup or something. Maybe he works in a circus like a clown or a traveling fish show or whatever—or maybe I just imagined the whole thing! 'Cause I've been sick. I'm delirious. That's what it is. I'm not a fish, I'm delirious."

The towels on his body were dry again, so he reached over to wet them in a bucket his mom had put by his bed.

"People get fevers all the time."

He draped the wet towels over his legs.

"And when they do, their bodies dry out and the skin on their legs gets all scaly like mine."

He put the last of the towels over his feet and lay back, having successfully convinced himself that he was normal. He was a normal sick boy.

He lay there for a moment . . . then . . . slowly thought, *"Scaly like mine?"*

He sat up carefully in his bed, lifted the towels above his knees, and peeked in.

He stared at his legs for a long time.

CHAPTER NINE

"**M**OM!! MOM!!" Morgan tried to yell, but it only sounded like a muffled moo.

He looked around for something to throw, but he couldn't reach anything. Then he remembered his scully-caps that were under his bed. They were in an old Wonder bread plastic bag. Scully-caps are bottle caps that you fill with melted crayons to give them more weight. You use them to play a game sort of like marbles—you just flick bottle caps instead.

He reached down and grabbed them and flung them at the bedroom door. They hit with a loud smack, and the caps scattered around the room as they fell. His mother rushed in.

"What's the matter, honey?"

"Ook aeh ai eggs."

"Cook you some eggs? Sure, I can—"

"Oh, oh! Ai eggs! Ai eggs!" he said again, this time throwing the covers off his legs.

Morgan's mother stared at his legs.

Expressionless.

His left leg, from mid thigh down to his ankle, was spotted with something that definitely looked kind of . . . scaly. Little dime-sized half-moons of a sort of silvery white were speckled about in oddly shaped patches. They were thickest right below the knee and mid calf, where they started to overlap one another, like shingles on a roof. His right leg was a bit more spotty, with just a few patches on his upper thigh and ankle.

His mother carefully ran her fingers down his leg.

So did Morgan.

The patches felt smooth and glossy, but kind of dry. When he ran his fingers back up toward his knee, they felt hard and raspy, like sandpaper.

Very calmly, his mother pulled the covers over his legs.

"I'll be right back," she said soothingly, and headed out the door.

The next thing Morgan knew, his mother was jumping up and down, stomping on the kitchen floor for Mrs. Pasalaqua.

His father started screaming, "What's going on?"

His mother kept stomping but she was dialing too. And then she was yelling into the phone.

Mrs. Pasalaqua was bounding up the stairs.

"WHAT'S GOING ON!?" screamed his father.

Just then something popped in Morgan's ear.

It was like when your ears pop in an airplane, but a hundred times louder. His head felt light as a feather, and he heard a soft, steady hum. Then there was a tremendous swooshing sound, like someone sucking up the last sips of a malted through a straw. It was horribly loud, like the straw was stuck right into his ear and was sucking something out of him, pulling at him—then there was another loud pop and . . . he could hear again.

But it was different.

It was just like when he was underwater in the bathtub.

He could hear everything as if it were amplified a hundred times. It was all a clamoring mess because he heard it all at the same time: the cars on the street, TVs in other apartments in the building, sirens screaming, horns honking, telephones ringing, the subway four blocks away, along with a thousand other sounds, and over it all his mother and father yelling in the kitchen. It hurt to listen. Morgan threw a pillow over his head and squeezed it around his face and ears.

Mrs. Pasalaqua let herself into the apartment. "No more stomp. I'ma here."

"He's worse," Mom said to Mrs. Pasalaqua, stopping stomping. "Come out in the hall."

Morgan strained to hear what they were saying above the din of all the other noises that were bombarding him. That was when he discovered that if he concentrated on one sound, really hard, if he really focused, he could kind of shut out most of the other noises. He couldn't do it for long, though. The voices in the hall kept going in and out, like a radio station that he couldn't quite tune in. But when it worked, when he tuned in on them, it was clearer than any sound he'd ever heard. It was as if someone had put a micro-phone in the hall, and the speaker was right next to his ear.

Morgan tried to tune in the whispered

conversation in the hall. He could understand most of it.

"Somebody tell me what—" his father said.

"Shh," shushed his mother. "He'll hear you."

"You call nine one one, yes?" Mrs. Pasalaqua asked his mother.

"I just did. They're on their way."

"Would somebody just tell me what's going on?!" his father yelled in a loud whisper.

"Shh!" scolded Mrs. Pasalaqua. "Where'sa the boy?" she asked Mom.

"In his room."

"You like I look?"

"His legs . . ." Mom tried to explain. "They look . . . kind of like scales."

"Scales?" Mrs. Pasalaqua and his father said.

"Yes, *scales*!"

"I look."

Morgan could hear the ambulance three blocks away.

"How'sa my little friend?" Mrs. Pasalaqua asked, coming into Morgan's room. "I like so much you, I come back, yes?" She sat next to him on the bed. "So, let me see what so much fuss your mother make about. Okay?"

Morgan lifted back the sheets again, revealing his legs.

Mrs. Pasalaqua stared silently for a moment. Her forehead wrinkled up into skinny furrows, and she bit the corner of her bottom lip. She leaned in close for a moment, paused, and then sat as far back in her chair as she could, straining to get a better view.

Suddenly her face relaxed and brightened. The furrows disappeared, and a thin smile crept across her lips. She nodded her head and crossed her arms with assurance.

"Yup, that'sa scales," she said, patting his leg.

"They're here!" Mom yelled from the kitchen. "They're coming down the block!"

"Company," Mrs. Pasalaqua said teasingly to Morgan. "Not to be scared, yes? They take-a good care of you. I make-a sure."

Morgan heard the ambulance screech to a stop in front of the wrong apartment building. His father screamed out the window at them. The sirens were blaring.

"Morgan?" his mother said, coming back into his room. "We're going to go to the hospital now, okay?"

Morgan squirmed and thrashed a *"No"* as

the paramedics came clattering and banging up the stairs. They barged into the apartment and came running into Morgan's room. Morgan grabbed the great silvery hook off his night table and held on to it. His mother and father hovered in the doorway, watching.

"How long has he had a temperature like this?" asked one of the paramedics.

"Since last night," his mother answered.

"Let's get him out of here," the paramedic said with authority. "Can he walk?"

"Can you walk, honey?" his mother asked softly.

"Of course I can walk." Morgan nodded as he stood up and fell on the floor. The paramedic went to help him, but Morgan's father stepped in.

"I got him," his father said. He picked Morgan up in his arms. "Get my coat," he told Mrs. Pasalaqua as he carried Morgan out of the apartment and down the three flights of stairs.

"How you doing?" his father whispered to Morgan halfway down, "You okay?"

"Mghmgh," Morgan mghmghed with a shrug of his shoulders. He felt small in his father's arms, and safe, like when he was a little boy and his dad used to carry him down to the corner newsstand on Sunday mornings, like he used to feel a long time ago.

"OPEN THE DOOR ALREADY!" his father shouted as he carried him to the ambulance.

"Thank you, we'll take it from here," the paramedic said to his father. "Please?"

His father backed away from the ambulance.

"Who's riding with us?" the driver shouted.

Morgan's mother looked around and, for just an instant, looked very lost.

"You go with him," his father said, touching her elbow. "I'll take the car and meet you there. Everything'll be fine."

His mother got in the back of the ambulance with Morgan. The paramedics buckled him in and strapped him down.

"Everything'll be fine," Mom reassured Morgan. "Everything'll be fine."

CHAPTER TEN

MORGAN SQUINNIED his eyes shut as his gurney was bumped through the hospital doors. It was too bright inside. There were lights everywhere. The receptionist looked up from her paperwork for a brief moment and threw a sideways glance at him as they wheeled him by. So did all the other people who were waiting in the emergency-room lobby. Morgan thought they all looked kind of upset because he was going to be seen by the doctors before they were. He hung his head off the side of the gurney and looked at them upside down, thinking, "Well, if *your* mouths were stuck shut, and *your* legs were covered with scales, then you could all go first. That would suit me just fine."

"Settle down!" one of the paramedics barked as he pressed Morgan's head back on the gurney and pushed him through a swinging door. Morgan flip-flopped his head from side to side, trying to see where he was and where he was going. All he could see was a blur of hallway walls and an occasional nurse whizzing past him. The paramedics pushed him through one more set of swinging doors, and the lights got brighter still.

"They should just give you sunglasses when you check in."

He was in a small room with huge lights hanging from various parts of the ceiling. The paramedics pushed his gurney up along one of the walls and locked the wheels.

"Somebody'll be right in," a paramedic said, backing out the door.

"Wait a minute!" Morgan tried to say, forgetting that his mouth wasn't working right. "Eight uh innu!" came out instead.

He didn't like being left alone in the room.

There was an examining table in the middle, and all along the walls were scary-looking machines that Morgan didn't even want to think about.

But he did.

He began imagining what each machine might do to what part of his body. Some of them had small lights that flickered on and off in strange patterns, and others made weird noises. They seemed to be alive.

Morgan knew he had to get out of the room, but he was still buckled down tight to the gurney. He tried to wriggle out. Then he leaned over the side as far as he could, but he was stuck. He hung there for a second, feeling the blood rush to his head and staring at the floor.

"Bats do this all the time."

The doors to the room swung open, and someone's legs walked in. Morgan could see big black shoes and the bottom of a lab coat between the struts of the gurney. The shoes turned left, then right, then straight ahead again as the doors flapped shut behind them. Then the legs squatted down, and there was a doctor peering at Morgan.

"Oh, there you are," he said. "You look a little blue."

Morgan tried to pull himself up onto the gurney but couldn't. The doctor came over and helped him up.

"There we go. Watch your head."

He looked just like doctors are supposed to

look, only the backs of his hands were extremely hairy.

"He should shave those things," Morgan thought.

The swinging doors swung open again, and four more people came in. Morgan's eyes leaped back and forth among the different faces that suddenly filled the room.

"Everyone to this side, please," said the doctor who was dressed like a doctor. They huddled together in the corner, peeking over one another's shoulders at Morgan with eager eyes.

"Everyone, this is Morgan," he said to the group.

"Hello, Morgan," they all said back, some on tiptoes.

Morgan eyed them.

"Ehhoh," he mumbled, suspiciously.

"So, how are we doing?" asked the doctor.

"Ai oheh," Morgan said with a shrug.

"Good. I'm Doctor Reichart," he said, unstrapping Morgan. "These other people are medical students." He gestured to the crowd in the corner.

Morgan looked over at them. They all smiled at him, and a few raised their arms halfway up and waved.

"They're here to watch me on my rounds and study what I do."

"Great," thought Morgan, feeling like a frog in biology class.

"Let's see how that fever is doing," said Dr. Reichart as he aimed a thermometer at Morgan's mouth. "Open," he asked with a friendly smile.

"Ai aien oen ai ouuh," Morgan tried to explain. *(I can't open my mouth.)*

"Open," the doctor said again with a bigger smile.

"Ai aien."

"It won't hurt at all," he insisted, the corners of his smile beginning to twitch.

Morgan tried to burn a hole in the doctor's forehead with the look he gave him.

"Sometimes younger patients are uneasy with certain procedures," the man intoned as he spun away from Morgan and addressed the group in the corner. "There's more than one way to take a temperature, as you all know."

They all laughed a snickery little laugh while they feverishly scratched down notes on their clipboards.

"Chart please," Dr. Reichart asked over his shoulder as he peered at Morgan. An anonymous arm with a manila folder attached to it shot out from the clump in the corner.

"Thank you."

Dr. Reichart opened the folder and flipped through a few pages with his hairy hands. He *hmm*ed a bit, and *aha*ed twice, peering at Morgan each time. Then he was silent for a moment. The students all stopped scribbling and waited to see what he would do next. He held the chart out behind him without looking, and the anonymous arm shot out again and snatched it back. He pulled on a pair of rubber gloves and walked toward the gurney.

"Well, this shouldn't take too long," he said very matter-of-factly as he lifted the covers off Morgan's legs. "It seems all we have is a simple case of—"

The clump in the corner gasped and seemed to get taller.

They squeezed and clung to each other so tightly now that Morgan thought they looked like one big person. Dr. Reichart stood silent with the corner of the covers still in his hand. He covered Morgan's legs again, turned to the clump, and said, "Would you please excuse us for a moment."

It scampered out of the room, like an enormous centipede.

Dr. Reichart lifted the covers again.

Both legs were completely covered with scales.

Morgan pushed himself up on both elbows to get a good look. There were scales everywhere.

Both legs.

And they were getting bigger. Some of them were the size of quarters now, and everywhere they overlapped each other. Morgan twisted to get a better view, and as he did, they glistened under the bright lights of the examining room. Each scale looked as if it had been sprinkled with millions of tiny silver-blue sparkles, and whenever Morgan moved, they glittered and flashed. Doctor Reichart winced his eyes away from the glare and quickly shut off some of the overhead lights. He stared at Morgan's legs. His eyes were as big as half dollars.

Morgan couldn't help but think his legs looked pretty neat. It was like wearing a beautiful suit of magical armor. Dr. Reichart got out a magnifying glass and a small metal probe. He started poking around at Morgan's legs. He scraped, and scratched, and tapped at the scales. They made a soft, hollowish noise. He lifted one of them up and tried to peer under it, but Morgan squirmed under him.

"Uou." *(Ow.)*

Dr. Reichart stopped. He stood up and walked backward, almost in slow motion, never taking his eyes off Morgan's legs. He stopped walking backward when he ran into the door. Through the windows of the door, to either side of Dr. Reichart's head, Morgan could see the students' faces crowding into one another in an effort to get a look into the room.

"It's true," Morgan thought. "I'm changing. I'm actually—" He stopped. The thought scared him.

Dr. Reichart banged on the door behind him. A head slid in.

"Call Dr. Keegan and Dr. Ashley."

The head slid back out and scurried through the students still massed outside the room.

Dr. Reichart pushed the door open farther and called out more instructions.

"And get me the duty nurse. Now!"

Dr. Reichart started preparing Morgan to be moved somewhere else. He buckled the straps across Morgan's arms and waist, wheeled the gurney around, and pointed it at the door. The nurse entered, and Dr. Reichart passed off Morgan to the nurse with a little shove. The nurse caught the gurney as it rolled across the room and continued pushing it, feet first, out the door. Dr. Reichart ran alongside, talking into a cellular phone that was squished between his shoulder and his ear. He was looking through a big black book. A crowd of people outside the doors parted to let them through. Morgan spotted his father popping his head up and down, trying and get a look.

"I'm *on* page eighty-five!" Dr. Reichart yelled into the phone. "*Eighty*-five, yes!"

"Excuse me," said Morgan's father from the back of the crowd.

"Which book do you have? No, what *year*?" Dr. Reichart continued into the phone.

"Excuse me. I'm Morg—" Morgan's father put his shoulder down and pushed through the gawkers, pulling his wife along behind him. "I'm Morgan's father. Where are you taking him?"

"Oh. You— One moment," the doctor said.

He put the big black book down on Morgan's gurney. He whispered into the phone, "I'll call back. See what you can find out." He turned to Morgan's parents. "He doesn't seem to be in any immediate danger," the doctor began. "All his vital signs are good, but he's extremely dehydrated. We're going to get him on an I.V. to get his fluids back to normal."

"What about those things on his legs?" asked his mother.

"Well, I don't exactly know just yet. I'm bringing in a couple of specialists I know. One is a dermatologist and the other is a surgeon."

"A surgeon!?" cried his mother, clutching Morgan's gurney. "What do you mean, a surgeon!?"

"It may not require any kind of surgical procedure." The doctor tried to make his voice sound soothing. "First we have to determine exactly what they are." He looked down at Morgan, and his eyes seemed to light up a little. "To be honest with you, I've never seen anything like it before."

CHAPTER ELEVEN

"**M**GOUGH!" SHOUTED MORGAN as the nurse stuck an I.V. needle into his arm.

"Sorry," she said, taping it in place so it wouldn't fall out.

The needle had a rubbery tube coming out of it that snaked over Morgan's head and ran up into a bag filled with some kind of liquid.

"I'm sure your parents will be here soon," the nurse reassured Morgan as she re-bobby-pinned her cap, which kept slipping sideways. "The doctors are just getting some—darn these stupid hats—they're just getting some information from them." Morgan handed her the bobby pin that fell out of her mouth and onto his gurney.

"Thanks," she said, capped again. "How do I look?"

"Oheh."

"Oh, you're a sweetie. Thanks. They make

us wear these things." She unbuckled the strap across Morgan's waist. "There we go. That must feel a little better, huh?"

"Eah."

The nurse dropped a hospital gown on Morgan's lap. "I'll turn my back while you slip that on. I'm Molly," she said, facing the wall. "This room is temporary. We'll get you another room later. With a TV. We're just waiting on Dr. Keegan and Dr. Ashley." She pulled the curtains on the window closed.

While Morgan was slipping the gown on, he peeked at his legs again. He wanted to make sure this was all really happening.

This was all really happening.

The scaly things were still there. He twisted his legs gently back and forth and watched the light bounce off them in streaks of prismed colors. Splatterings of colored light danced on the wall next to the curtain that Molly was closing. Morgan saw her look up at them.

"Oh, isn't that pretty. What are you playing with?" she asked, turning back. "Is it a—? Oh, my goodness. Would you look at that."

Her mouth slid down to one side and her little cap slid down the other. She was still holding the edge of the curtain in her hand.

"Why don't we just—uh . . ." She made her way toward the gurney with her weight slightly on the backs of her heels. "—uh . . . put those sheets back. Yeah, that's what we'll do." She pulled the sheets back over his legs. "I'm, uh . . . I'm going to go see where everyone is, okay? Now why don't you—"

Her cap fell off her head again. She made a quick attempt to grab it, bobbled it for a moment, and missed.

"Don't you worry about a thing. No, sir. I'll be right back," she said apologetically as she squeezed out the door.

The only thing left of Molly was her little cap in the middle of the floor.

Morgan unclasped his hands and looked at the great silvery hook he'd been holding on to the whole time. He reached over and put it in the drawer of the table next to his bed.

Morgan held his arms up and looked at them in the light. They looked fine to him. A little dry, but fine. Quickly he pulled up his shirt and looked at his belly and chest.

Nothing.

He looked under his arms, around his

elbows, and in between his fingers. Everything looked okay. Nothing else seemed to be changing. He tried bending his knees and ankles. They moved okay. The scales overlapped and dovetailed perfectly under and over one another no matter which way he turned. He could barely even feel them. It felt like his skin.

On the corner of the gurney was the big black book. Dr. Reichart had left it there when he'd run into Morgan's parents. Morgan sat himself up all the way and reached over for it. When he leaned forward, something caught on the back of his gown.

Something from the gurney was stuck on the back of his gown. Morgan pulled himself free and turned around to see what it was.

There was nothing there.

"Weird."

He leaned forward to grab the book and, again, something grabbed the back of his gown. He reached around to yank whatever it was free, but couldn't find anything. Then he spun around as fast as he could to try to catch whatever it was. Nothing.

Then he had a thought.

Slowly he reached his hand around his

back. He felt between his shoulder blades and along his sides. He kept his eyes closed, straightened himself up, and felt as much of his back as he could. Then he switched hands, but he couldn't feel as far with the other one because it had the I.V. in it. But still he felt nothing. That was scary. For a second he thought that maybe— He felt something.

He leaned forward again. His hand was still on the small of his back when he leaned forward, and as he did, he felt something spring up. Something sharp. He quickly sat up straight again and felt for it, but it was gone. He felt all over. It was gone.

Next time, he started leaning forward slowly and kept his hand in the middle of his back. Halfway into the lean he felt it again. He stopped mid lean.

Something pointy, like a row of soft spikes, was running down the entire length of his back.

It had gently sprung up right under his hand in the middle of leaning forward. He tried to run his hand up his back, but he couldn't. His hand stuck on whatever they were. They were like little teeth that were angled down and could be stroked only one way. He crept his hand up along the outside of his back and then felt from the top of his shoulders down. His hand slid right over the spikes as if they weren't even there. He could barely feel them. It was like they had retracted right into his back.

Morgan wanted to look in a mirror but was too scared to get off the gurney. He didn't exactly know what it would feel like if a human being were to grow a dorsal fin, but he could guess that it would probably feel something like this.

"Do you hear yourself?!" he yelled in his head. "This is crazy! There's a logical explanation for all of this. There has to be. *The book* . . . I'll bet it's in the book."

He grabbed the big black book that was on the end of the gurney and dragged it up on his scaly knees.

A Guide to Dermatohistopathology.

"Doesn't sound good," he thought.

He flopped the big pages open and turned to the sections that Dr. Reichart had dog-eared.

Atopic Dermatitis . . . Psoriasis . . . Keratosis . . .

The pictures were disgusting. All kinds of

horrible skin diseases were pictured next to some of the names.

Eczema . . . Fungal and Viral Infections of the Skin . . .

Nothing looked anything like what was on Morgan's legs. Whatever he had was definitely pretty strange, but it surely wasn't as nasty as these things.

Ichthyosis and Its Genetic Predispositions: A Theory.

The door opened, and Morgan instinctively flopped back on the gurney. He didn't want anyone seeing whatever it was that was on his back. Everyone thought he was weird enough as it was.

He expected the doctors to come barging in, but it was his mother who poked her head inside the room.

"Hey, there." She smiled.

She opened the heavy door a little more, and behind her was his father, who waved, and behind him was Mrs. Pasalaqua. Behind them all were Molly and the clump of medical students.

His mother gave him a big hug. "The doctors are going to come up and do a few tests to find out what's going on. Okay?"

"We'll stay here till they show up," his father added.

"Yes, righta here we stay." Mrs. Pasalaqua sat on a chair and crossed her arms. "We don'ta go nowhere."

His mother went and pulled the window curtains open. It was pitch black outside except for a little toenail clip of a moon.

There was a terribly awkward silence.

Finally Mrs. Pasalaqua broke it by saying, "You know, where I come-a from, you cana no slaughter a pig in the full moon."

Morgan had no idea what she meant by that.

CHAPTER TWELVE

THE OTHER DOCTORS didn't arrive until the next morning. They asked everyone to leave the room.

"Nurse," one called out behind her as she came in the door.

Molly scuffled in and scooped up her cap, which was still on the floor. She shut the curtains again and turned back to escort the family out the door. The doctors were in the corner huddled up and conferring about something.

Dr. Reichart came into the room.

"Morning, everyone. Good morning, Morg— There it is," he said, spotting the big black book on the end of Morgan's gurney. He grabbed it and turned into the huddle, flipping through the pages. The huddle bent toward the book with great interest. Dr. Reichart was reading short passages out loud every now and then, and showing pictures to the other doctors.

After Molly had seen everyone out of the room, she came back and stood against the wall. She still had one hand on her head when Morgan looked over at her. She winked at him while she wrestled with her cap. It was winning again.

"Would you excuse us," Dr. Reichart said to Molly. He didn't look up from the huddle. "Excuse us," he said again.

"But—"

He looked up.

Molly left the room.

The huddle broke open, and the three doctors looked at Morgan. They approached him cautiously. Dr. Reichart took the lead and pushed Morgan's gurney alongside an examining table in the center of the room.

"Why don't you just scoot up here for us, Morgan. Can you do that?"

Morgan shimmied over onto the white-papered examining table, keeping himself covered with the sheets from the gurney.

"This is Dr. Keegan and Dr. Ashley," Dr. Reichart continued. "They're going to take a look at your legs. Okay?"

Dr. Reichart pulled back the sheets.

Morgan could see that Dr. Keegan and Dr. Ashley were trying hard not to look surprised, even though they were. Dr. Reichart gave them both a look, like "See? I told you so." They circled and studied. First they acted as a group; then, after gaining confidence, they split up and each started doing their own thing.

"Hello there," Dr. Keegan said while he examined Morgan. "How are we doing today?"

Dr. Keegan was the dermatologist. He specialized in skin diseases. He was pretty short for a doctor, Morgan thought. His head barely came over the examining table. He kept his hands in his pockets and scrunched up his shoulders around his ears. His curly head paced up and down alongside Morgan's legs, stopping every once in a while to take a closer look.

Dr. Ashley, the surgeon, had brought her own tools with her. They were in a small plastic pouch that looked like one of those eyeglass screwdriver sets you can buy at checkout counters. Her hair was pulled back and up into a tight bun on the top of her head. It was so tight, it looked like it hurt her face, and it stretched her lips into a kind of tiny fake smile all the time. She pulled out a gadget that looked like a skinny potato peeler and leaned over Morgan's knee. She started scraping something from one of the scales onto a small piece of glass. She was very quiet and extremely freckled. Everywhere. Morgan wondered which part of her was freckle and which wasn't—like zebras. Are they white with black stripes or black with white stripes? She picked and poked at the scales with tools that Morgan had never seen before. Then she pried at his lips, but they wouldn't budge. She felt under his jaw, pushed in his cheeks, and wiggled his nose. She couldn't get his mouth to open. She wrote something down on a clipboard and went back to examining the scales.

"MGOUGH!" Morgan shouted as one of the pokes hurt him.

"Sorry," said Dr. Ashley. "I'm going to run these to the lab," she continued to Dr. Reichart, who was still studying the big black book.

"It's not in there," Morgan thought. "There's nothing about this in there."

Dr. Ashley bustled out the door. Dr. Keegan's little head was now pacing around the entire examining table.

"Does anybody think to ask *me* what the problem is?" Morgan thought. "No."

The next time Dr. Keegan circled by, Morgan reached over and snatched a pen from his pocket. He tore a piece off of the crinkly white paper that was laid out under him on the examining table and wrote a note to Dr. Reichart.

"Aaor" *(Doctor)*, Morgan said, waving the note.

Nobody heard him.

"AAOR!" he said again, throwing the pen at Dr. Reichart and holding up the note.

"Yes?" said the doctor, coming over. Morgan handed him the note. Dr. Reichart read it and then handed it to Dr. Keegan.

They both left the room.

Morgan scratched his belly. He listened to the I.V. drip-dropping into his arm, and the machine in the corner humming softly. If he concentrated, he could listen to the voices all the way down the hall. He only had to sort of think about which sound he wanted to listen to, and the other noises would fade away. He could also smell things that he had never smelled before: doctors' rubber gloves, perfumes and colognes out in the hall, food from the cafeteria two floors above, exhaust from cars in the street; and if he concentrated really hard, he thought he could even smell his father's cigar being smoked somewhere outside. And if he concentrated even harder, he could let himself think of how wonderful it would be if a person could actually change into a marlin. If a person could—

"People don't turn into marlins, you dope!" he thought, cutting himself off.

He scratched his belly again.

CHAPTER THIRTEEN

THE NEXT MORNING Morgan was moved to another room. He was lying on his side thinking about the old man—the old *marlin*—whom he had seen, for that's what Morgan believed now, that the man was somehow some part . . . marlin. He didn't know how or why, he couldn't explain it or make anyone else understand it, but he believed that there was something unspeakably strange and wonderful going on. He remembered how the man had known his name and spoken to him, how his voice had hummed through his body, and how his eyes had been of another world. Something had happened to that man. And now something was happening to Morgan.

And it was real.

No matter how many times Morgan thought he would open his eyes and it would all be gone, like that Sunday afternoon when all this started, it wasn't.

It was still there.

And whatever it was that was growing out of Morgan's back was getting more uncomfortable all the time. If he didn't lie perfectly straight, the spiny things would start to poke out all over the place. When he curled up on his side, he could feel them spring up and push out the back of his hospital gown. It felt good when he did that. Sort of like a good stretch feels, or a yawn.

That afternoon Molly poked her capless head in the door, and Morgan quickly flipped onto his back.

"Oh, it's just me. I told your mom I'd sneak up and look in on you," she said as she checked his I.V. "Mom and Dad are down in the lobby, and your friend Mrs. Pakasockwa is there too. She's a funny one." Molly adjusted the pillows. "Now look at you. You look stiff as a board lying there like that. Want me to raise the back of the bed so you can sit up for a while?"

"Oh!" he said quickly, meaning *No!*

"Oh what, dear?"

"Uh-uh," he said this time, shaking his head no.

"No? Well, let me show you how to do it in

104

case you want to later. You just push this little button here," she said, pushing the button.

"Oh! OH! Uh-uh!"

"Oh, oh! Yes, I know, it's kind of fun, isn't it?"

The spiny things running along Morgan's back started to pop out as the bed rose.

"And this one's for the TV," Molly said, pushing another box of buttons and looking up at the screen. "Oh, look at the junk they put on today."

The bed kept rising.

"Let me find you something good to watch." She paused at a soap opera.

The fin kept finning. It felt bigger than before. Long spikes billowed out the back of Morgan's blue hospital gown and pushed him forward.

"Oh, forget it," Molly said, turning off the TV. "There's nothing on this time of—"

Morgan was bent over double, his nose almost touching his knees.

"Oh, well, dear, guess that's a bit too much, huh?"

Molly pushed another button, and the bed slowly fell back down. Morgan straightened himself out and felt the finny thing on his back retract. He smoothed his hospital gown under him and scratched his belly.

"What, you got an itch there? Those sheets bothering you?"

"Uh-uh. Ai ine."

"Really?"

"Eely."

"Okay, well don't be shy. You just speak up if you want anything."

"Oheh."

Dr. Reichart walked into the room.

"Would you excuse us?" he asked like he was annoyed.

"Oh, of course. On my way out," Molly answered, turning to Morgan. "If you need anything, you buzz the thingajigga, okay? Right there by your bed. I'll check up on you again later—"

"Nurse."

"Leaving."

"Nurse."

"Yes, doctor?"

"Where's your hat?"

"My—oh, my hat. Yes, I . . . Well, it's right out—"

"Put it on."

"Yes, sir. Right away."

Molly hurried out the door. Something

about Molly made Morgan want to smile.

"Hello, Morgan."

Something about Dr. Reichart didn't make him want to smile.

"Ehhoh."

"I just wanted to drop by to tell you . . ." He picked up the sheets and looked at Morgan's legs as he talked. "Hmm . . . to tell you . . . that there's someone here to see you. Dr. Hanson. She'd like to talk to you. All right?"

"Ot ah ai ouua ei . . . oh?" *(What am I gonna say . . . no?)*

"Good . . . good . . ." Dr. Reichart dropped the sheets back onto Morgan's legs. "I'm sure you'll like her."

Dr. Reichart opened the door and let in Dr. Hanson. She was taller than Dr. Reichart and wearing something around her neck that looked like a ribbon with a brooch attached to it. To Morgan it looked like a dog collar. The brooch was black and so big that she had to hold her chin permanently up to be comfortable. It looked like she had whiplash. The ribbon was black too. As a matter of fact, everything she was wearing was black. Except for the fat silver bracelets she wore that jangled and clanked whenever she moved.

"I'll leave you two alone," Dr. Reichart said as he closed the door.

"Hi there," said Dr. Hanson as she jing-jangled toward him.

"Ehhoh."

She pulled a chair over to Morgan's bed and shimmied up close to him, clanking with each shimmy.

"So. I'm Helen Hanson. You can call me Dr. Hanson. *(Clank-clink.)* I'm the resident psychologist here, and I'd like to ask you a few questions, okay?"

"Oheh," answered Morgan warily. He fingered a bag she had plopped on his bed.

"First off—don't touch that please. I'd like to begin with—please don't touch! I'll take that." She snatched the bag away from Morgan and dug into it. *(Clinkety-cling.)* "This is for you." She pulled out a small chalkboard and a piece of chalk and handed them to Morgan with a jingle. "If you need to say anything, just write on there. Yes? All right."

She searched around inside her bag for something else. Morgan was staring at her eyebrows. She didn't have any. They were fake. There was nothing there but black lines that were drawn with some kind of a makeup pencil thing. The lines were absolutely perfectly even.

"Now, *that's* weird," Morgan thought. "Who would shave their eyebrows?"

"Here we go," she said, pulling out the crumpled-up piece of paper that Morgan had given to Dr. Reichart earlier. "This is yours, isn't it? All right, let's just see what we have here." She slowly uncrumpled the piece of paper, jingling and clinking as she did, and read it to Morgan.

"I AM A MARLIN. *(Clink.)* Did you write that?"

Morgan nodded yes.

"You did. Okay. Now what does that mean to you?"

"Hmm?"

"What does that—Are you a gang member? Is this some sort of—"

Morgan shook his head no.

"—sort of club with initiation rites or . . ."

He kept shaking his head *no*.

"Did someone do this to you?"

Morgan took the chalkboard and wrote in big letters: A MARLIN IS A FISH. He held it up to her.

"I know that. But your little note here says that—"

He wrote again and held up the board. It said: TURNING INTO ONE.

"What's turning?"

Morgan pointed to himself.

"You . . . what, you're what?"

He held up the same words: TURNING INTO ONE.

"You're turning into one."

Morgan nodded his head yes.

"A . . . fish."

He wrote again: A <u>MARLIN</u>. BIG DIF-FERENCE!

"Morgan . . . Morgan, people cannot turn into—"

Morgan pulled back the sheets and showed Dr. Hanson his legs.

"Oh oh?" *(Oh no?)* he said.

She looked over her chin at them and was amazingly unimpressed.

"Yes. So?"

"Ot ou oo een, 'Oh?' . . . Ai oah aels awn ai eggs!" *(What do you mean, "So?" . . . I've got scales on my legs!)*

"Morgan . . . I don't want to be the one to disappoint you, but Dr. Reichart has briefed me on your case. It seems you have something similar to a disease called ichthyosis. One of its symptoms is actually the growth of scales very similar to what you have. Ichthyosis, however, is very rare and generally inherited from your parents. There's no history of this disease in your family, so we're pretty sure what you have is more on the lines of your basic fungal infection. In the same family as athlete's foot."

For some reason Morgan felt exactly the same way as when Mrs. McSwiggen stood him up in front of the greenboard full of math problems. He felt flushed all over, embarrassed, and extremely small.

"Now, I'm going to recommend that we have a few little sessions together. Just to talk about these . . . these *thoughts* you have. Imagination is one thing, but when you're sick like this, it can sometimes lead to psychosomatic complications of the—"

Morgan interrupted Dr. Hanson by handing her another message he had written on the chalkboard. It said:

HOW'S THIS FOR ATHLETE'S FOOT!

As soon as she read it, Morgan tore off his hospital robe and leaned forward on the bed. As he did, the spikes on his back sprang out with a loud swoosh, catching both pillows with their sharp barbs and flinging them halfway across the room. Starting at the base of his neck and running down the length of his back, the different-sized spikes ran from smallest right near his neck, maybe two inches, to one that was almost a foot long right between his shoulder blades. Then they started to get smaller and taper off as they neared the small of his back. In between the spikes was now a thin, filmy membrane connecting each one to the next.

Dr. Hanson did not move from her chair, but her painted eyebrows flew up. Morgan straightened his back, and the fin disappeared like a lady's fan that you fold up with a quick flick of your wrist. He bent his back again, fanned out his fin, and shook it from side to side. It made a bit of a wind that mussed up Dr. Hanson's hair. It also seemed to wake her up, for she suddenly leaped out of her chair with a scream and bolted out the door. Morgan listened to her jingle-jangle and clank all the way down the hall.

He straightened himself, closed up his fin, and lay back on the bed.

"Athlete's foot!" he said to himself.

Morgan didn't feel small anymore.

He felt huge.

CHAPTER FOURTEEN

DR. REICHART CAME bursting into the room, leaving a trail of med students behind.

Morgan pretended he was asleep.

Outside the doors he could hear the students shuffling about and Dr. Hanson jingle-jangling at some safe distance far away from the room. Dr. Reichart was out of breath. He checked the I.V. and Morgan's blood pressure, and took another look at Morgan's legs before gently turning Morgan over on his side. Morgan kept himself as straight as he could as the doctor turned him. Dr. Reichart slowly opened the back of the hospital gown. Morgan felt his cold hands searching around his back. Dr. Reichart's fingers poked and rubbed along the tiny ridge that ran down the center of his back.

Then Dr. Reichart stopped. His fingers changed directions and now made their way along Morgan's side. Morgan wondered what he was doing there, so he squinted his eyes open and peeked at the doctor. Under where his elbow lay against his side was an odd patch of color. Morgan watched as Dr. Reichart rubbed it with his hairy hands. It didn't look like scales at all. It looked . . . leathery. Morgan wondered what was going on, so he pretended to wake up. He faked a yawn and rolled onto his back, looking up at the doctor.

"Ai, Oc."

"Hi. Just lie still. I need to check a few things."

"Oheh."

"Let's just pull this gown up some more so I can get a look your belly."

"Ei eishes."

"What?"

IT ITCHES, he wrote on the chalkboard.

"I see. Okay, I'll see what I can—"

Morgan pulled his gown up. The small leathery patch that started on his side ran up and across his entire chest and down over his belly. It was a wrinkled white in the very middle of his belly and chest, then faded into a soft, grayish white as it spread out, and finally melted into an ashy blue at his waist and along his sides. Below his belly button it disappeared into the glittering silvery-blue scales that now went clear up around his hips. Dr. Reichart threw back the covers on his legs. Not only did they go clear around his hips, but the scales now went completely down both legs.

Morgan and Dr. Reichart both stared in silence.

Morgan slowly scribbled a note on the chalkboard and slid it down his bed toward the doctor. It read:

TOLD YOU SO.

"I need my . . . my book. I need my big book," Dr. Reichart said as he walked into the bathroom of Morgan's room thinking it was the door to the hallway.

"It's not in there," he said coming back out. "I'll be right back." As he opened the door, the med students schooled up again and waited for his next move.

"Nurse! Molly! MOLLY!!" he started calling.

The students started echoing the doctor and calling out too. "Molly! Nurse Molly!" they yelled down halls, behind desks, in the lobby, and over the intercom.

Finally, Molly appeared from the ladies' room right across the hall from where Morgan was. She paused in the doorway for a moment.

"Just a— one sec . . . I—" she said.

"Oh, forget the stupid hat! Come here!"

"Yes, doctor." She tossed her cap to a student.

"Stay here. No one in or out. No contact. Understand? No one."

"Yes, sir."

Dr. Reichart hurried away, and the students waddled off behind him. Molly closed the door and came into the room.

"He doesn't need to be so huffy all the time. Hi there."

"Ai."

"How we doing?"

"Oheh."

"Yeah, me too. Just okay. How's your legs doing?"

"Ook." He pulled back the covers.

"Goodness, look at you." She followed the glittering scales with her eyes. "You look like a treasure. Does it hurt?"

"Ot aeh aw." *(Not at all.)*

He covered his legs again and lifted his

hospital gown so she could see his stomach and chest.

"Oh, my. That's new, huh?"

Morgan nodded his head yes.

"Goodness. And you feel fine?"

"Ate. Ai eel ush ate." He wrote something on the chalkboard.

"Oh, what a good idea," she said of the chalkboard. "Why didn't I think of that?"

Morgan held up the board. Molly read it out loud.

"DO YOU BELIEVE I'M TURNING INTO A MARLIN?"

"What's a marlin, dear?"

Morgan wished he had the picture of the marlin that hung above his bed at home to show her. He couldn't imagine how anyone could describe a marlin. So he didn't try.

IT'S A KIND OF FISH, he wrote instead.

"A fish. Oh, yes, I heard someone say that." Molly checked a few things around the room as she continued talking. "There's so much gossip around the hospital. Not from me, though. A fish, huh? Well, they say we all came from fish to begin with; I don't see why it couldn't work the other way." She adjusted a

117

little knob on the I.V. "Only thing is . . . it took millions of years the first time, and *you* seem to be changing by the hour." She gently tucked him under the covers. "To be honest with you, Morgan, I don't know much about things like this. I just like to take care of people. But I know one thing." She held his head up and fluffed his pillow. "You must be a special person. 'Cause only special people have special things happen to them. You believe that?"

"Ai ouwn oh."

"Well, look at you there," she said. "All snugged up like a bug in a carpet—rug—you know what I mean."

Morgan smiled.

The door flew open and slammed against the wall behind it. In came three male orderlies and Dr. Reichart. They were all wearing white rubber gloves, and they had green masks over their mouths and noses.

"We're moving him," Dr. Reichart said, dismissing Molly.

The biggest orderly picked Morgan up and placed him on another gurney. Morgan kept himself stiff as a board when he moved him so he wouldn't fin out. Rubber gloves disconnected some things and reattached others, and before Morgan knew it, he was out of the room and being whisked down another long hallway.

"East wing," Dr. Reichart yelled after the orderlies. The biggest one, the one who had lifted Morgan onto the gurney, seemed to be in charge. He walked in front of the gurney, clearing the way, while the other two pushed. They took a quick left turn and headed to the elevator. They pushed him in, and Morgan lifted his head to see the doors slide shut on Molly and Dr. Reichart.

When the doors slid open again, two gloved and masked female nurses took the gurney from there—like a hospital relay team. The nurses chattered to each other across the gurney as they pushed Morgan down a long hallway that was lined with tinted windows. Then they banged through two very large swinging doors into a room that looked like a small gymnasium. It smelled like one too. They pushed him through this room and through the two huge doors on the opposite side, which opened into a dark corridor. One of the nurses was fumbling through a set of keys, trying to open a glass door that had something written on it. Morgan tried to read it but couldn't make it out. The other nurse was searching for the lights. Morgan pushed himself up a bit to see where he was, but he felt his fin start to sprout, so he dropped back down.

"Got 'em," said one of the nurses as she flipped on the lights.

"That'll help a little," said the nurse who was looking through dozens of keys. "Here we go." She unlocked the glass door and jammed it open with a wooden block that was there. "Give a hand here," she called to the other.

They pushed Morgan into the room, and as he was going through the doorway, he glanced up to see what was written on the glass door. It read:

HYDROTHERAPY

One of the nurses flipped on another light, and the room lit up. It was cavernous. A huge open room with four tremendous stainless-steel vats. The lights overhead hummed.

"The doctors will be here in a little bit," one of them said to Morgan. "Why don't you try to get a little sleep." The nurses went and sat in two chairs on the other side of the room.

Morgan wasn't even the littlest bit tired. His

mind raced. Yesterday he had just had a bunch of weird-looking scales on his legs, and now he was halfway to—

He stopped himself from thinking the rest of that thought.

Morgan flopped his head to the side and stared at the wall behind him. It was stainless steel too. He didn't like this room.

Something about it troubled him.

CHAPTER FIFTEEN

THERE WERE NO CLOCKS in the hydro-therapy room, and no windows to the outside. It was getting late, and Morgan wondered where his parents were. He was bored. He had a staring contest with the two nurses, but they were easy to beat, which bored him even more.

"Out! Get them out of here and down to quarantine!" Dr. Reichart yelled to his gang of orderlies, who stormed into the room with him.

They were all dressed in white jumpsuits, rubber gloves, and plastic hoods that covered their heads and faces. They reminded Morgan of those stupid astronaut costumes he always saw for sale around Halloween.

"Come on, get them out of here!"

The three spacemen roughly ushered the nurses out of the room. Dr. Reichart kicked the wooden block out from the bottom of the door, and it closed behind them. Morgan watched everyone fade and blur away through the thick glass. Everyone except Dr. Reichart. He stayed in the room.

"Hello, Morgan," Dr. Reichart said in a muffled voice through his plastic Halloween hood.

"Trick or treat," thought Morgan.

Dr. Reichart walked toward Morgan. His space suit made scrunchy noises every time he moved, like new corduroy pants.

"Now, don't let these suits scare you. It's just a precaution. We don't know if what you have is contagious, so we're just playing it safe for right now. We—"

Dr. Reichart's plastic hood began fogging up every time he talked. He tried to wipe off the clear plastic, but it was fogged up from the inside, and it didn't do any good. Dr. Reichart continued to wipe the front of it anyway. The only time it actually got any clearer was when he stopped talking. So every once in a while that was exactly what he did.

"We have your parents down in quarantine . . . along with Mrs. Pasalaqua. . . . Quarantine is just a safe place where they stay . . . and can't leave until we're . . . sure that whatever it is you have . . . is not contagious. They won't be able to see you for a . . . while. Not until we find out a little more about . . . what's going on here. I—"

Dr. Reichart broke off in the middle of whatever it was he was about to say. He ran to the far corner of the room and quickly pulled off the hood he was wearing. He wheezed and gasped and pulled in deep breaths of air, coughed a few times, and then tried to clean off the fogged-up mask with his sleeve.

He threw the mask on again and ran back over to Morgan. "Just wait here one moment. I'm going up there. Just wait." He rushed out of the room.

It was quiet for a moment, and then Morgan heard the doctor's voice on an intercom.

"Testing . . . one, two, three. . . . Testing. Hello. Hello to Morgan. This Dr. Reichart. Hello to Mor—"

"Ai eer oo!"

"Ah, good. Well . . . good. One moment . . . Let's see . . . ah, here we are." The doctor flipped on a bank of lights, and the entire upper third of the room lit up brightly, revealing a narrow glass booth that ran the entire length of the wall about ten feet up. A long line of computers and tops of microphones sat with their backs against the windows.

"Up here. Hi there. This is—"

The microphone went dead. Morgan could hear him just as well without it.

"This stupid . . . We spend all this money on these dumb— Just a— Testing . . . hello . . ." Suddenly the system came back on. The volume was set at ear shattering. "Testi— Ahh!" Quickly, the doctor lowered the volume and spoke very softly, very calmly into the microphone. "Sorry about that."

Dr. Keegan and Dr. Ashley joined Dr. Reichart in the booth.

"You can't even breathe in these things," Dr. Keegan complained from somewhere below the counter.

"I know. I know," Dr. Reichart said.

"And they fog up when you talk," added Dr. Ashley.

"Enough about the suits! What have you— Just a moment." Dr. Reichart went over to the microphone. "Morgan? I'm just going to turn this off for a second. We have to discuss a few things, and then we'll get right back to you."

"Oheh." Morgan nodded and concentrated so he could hear the conversation in the booth.

It was surprisingly easy.

"The biopsy came out negative," Dr. Ashley began. "As for it being contagious or not, I'll need more time. Until then we should maintain quarantine."

"Very well," said Dr. Reichart.

Dr. Keegan was next. "I've ruled out most of the known fungal infections."

"What about the lichenification of the torso?" asked Dr. Reichart.

"Well, it's reminiscent of psoriasis, atopic dermatitis—" said Dr. Keegan.

"Eczema." Dr. Ashley chimed in.

"But as I said, it's merely reminiscent of these diseases."

"What have we come up with about ichthyosis?"

Morgan remembered that word. Dr. Hanson had used it.

"Well, it's most common in children between one and four years old. It's extremely rare to have it appear in older children," Dr. Ashley stated.

"And," continued Dr. Keegan, "it's usually isolated to the elbows and knees. And sometimes the hands. Never to such an extent as we see here. And we can find no history of it in his family."

"Hmm."

"Hmm."

"Hmmm."

All three of them looked down at Morgan and continued talking. Morgan knew they were assuming he couldn't hear them. Morgan smiled at them and waved, listening to everything they said. They smiled back and continued talking to one another.

"The odd thing is, he's surprisingly healthy," Dr. Reichart mused.

"You heard about the note?" Dr. Reichart asked Dr. Ashley.

"Yes. Interesting."

"What do you make of it?"

"Was he raving?" Dr. Ashley asked Dr. Reichart.

"Well," Dr. Reichart considered. "He hit me with a pen."

"He wasn't raving," Dr. Keegan said, defending Morgan.

"Hmm . . . don't know then," she answered. "I spoke to the parents in quarantine. They did confirm an inordinate amount of the patient's time has recently been spent admiring fish." She looked in her notes. "Uh, *marlin*, that is. His mother said there's quite a big difference. That and his diet altered slightly. Craving canned anchovies."

"Allergic reaction to canned fish?" Dr. Keegan tossed up from below the counter.

"Unlikely," said Dr. Reichart.

"And what of Dr. Hanson's report?" asked Dr. Keegan.

"I gave him only a preliminary examination," answered Dr. Reichart. "I noticed nothing except some small raised ridges running down the spine—that's when I noticed the growth covering his torso. I think we're dealing with an extremely rare disease, something never recorded before now."

"I agree," agreed Dr. Ashley.

"We could be making history," added Dr. Reichart.

"History?" asked Dr. Keegan with a perky look.

"History."

All of them *hmm*ed.

"Okay, then. Next, treatments?"

"Well, they're very traditional. Lactic acid lotions—"

"Petroleum jelly wraps."

"Coal tar soaps, oil baths."

"Oil baths seem to have been the most successful in the past," agreed Dr. Reichart. "We must keep him moist. Every time I see him, he seems more dehydrated, no matter how much I.V. hydration he's taken in."

"Yes," said Dr. Keegan. "He does sort of respond like a dried-up fi—"

"Pardon?" asked Dr. Ashley.

"Don't say it," warned Dr. Reichart. "Oil bath it is."

Dr. Reichart leaned into the microphone and turned it on.

"Morgan? Sorry about that. Don't mean to be rude, but we had to talk about a few things."

Morgan shrugged his shoulders.

"Just relax," he continued, "and I'll explain to you exactly what we're going to do." He covered up the microphone with his hand and whispered down to Dr. Keegan. "We need a name for this. If we've discovered an unknown disease, I mean, if we've actually done that, there's a good chance we could get our names in, well, a medical journal!"

"Do you really think so?" asked Dr. Ashley with interest.

"Absolutely," said Dr. Reichart.

"A medical journal!" Dr. Ashley said to herself.

"We need a name! Quick, Dr. Ashley, look up—"

"I've taken the liberty," piped up Dr. Keegan.

"What?" they both asked.

"Of choosing a name. I've taken the liberty."

"You have?" asked Dr. Ashley.

"I have." Dr. Keegan pulled out a little memo book and read from it. *Makaira amplasitosis.*"

"Hmm . . . what does it mean? The root *Makaira ampla*?" asked Dr. Reichart.

"It's one of the old scientific names," said Dr. Keegan, "for the blue marlin."

Dr. Reichart and Dr. Ashley said the name to themselves a few times. Rolled the words around in their mouths like a piece of candy . . . relishing them.

"I like it," said Dr. Reichart.

"Yes. Well done," agreed Dr. Ashley.

"Makaira ampla . . ." Morgan said to himself. *"Makaira ampla."*

CHAPTER SIXTEEN

DR. REICHART HAD COME BACK down into the room with Dr. Keegan to explain to Morgan what was going on. Morgan felt sorry for Dr. Keegan, because they couldn't find a space suit that even came close to fitting him. He had doubled up his sleeves and wrapped them with big hospital-green rubber bands to hold them up. The bottoms of his pant legs were gathered up in big folds around his ankles, and big rubber bands held them up too. His hood kept slipping down over his eyes, and he had to keep pushing it back up.

Dr. Ashley stayed up in the booth, which was now filled with many other doctors and dozens of med students. Everyone was talking at the same time, and nobody was listening to anyone. They were all trying to give their opinion of what Morgan's condition might be. Morgan concentrated and tuned out the noise from above. It hurt his head to listen to them. It was easy to choose what to listen to now. It was just like turning speakers on and off. If he wanted to listen to the chatter up in the booth, he'd simply turn that speaker on and he could hear it.

"Morgan?" asked Dr. Reichart. "Morgan, can you hear me?"

"Only when I feel like it," Morgan thought as he nodded his head yes.

"Good."

"Hello, Morgan," said Dr. Keegan as he reached his little hand up on the gurney and patted Morgan's hand.

"Ehhoh."

Dr. Keegan began examining Morgan's belly and chest.

Through the glass door came one of Dr. Reichart's orderlies in his space suit. It was the big one. The Hulk. Spaceman. He didn't say anything to anyone, just walked over to one of the vats behind Morgan and began flipping switches and connecting tubes.

"Is he trained to speak?" Morgan wanted to ask, as he craned his head back to try to see exactly what Spaceman was doing. Suddenly, the tremendous groan of an engine waking up roared behind Morgan. It sputtered, kicked a little, and then coughed itself into a soft hum.

"That's just the hydrotherapy tank," Dr. Reichart reassured Morgan.

"That guy *looks* like a tank," Morgan thought.

Spaceman flipped another switch, and Morgan heard the sound of water crashing and gushing into the empty steel tank.

"We're going to let you take a long bath," Dr. Reichart explained. "We want to keep you moist until we decide how to remove the growths from your skin."

"Remove?" The thought jolted Morgan.

"We'll be applying some lotions to your body, and there's a kind of oil mixed in with the water. It'll be like a big bubble bath."

"Remove?"

"Before we do, though, let's have a look at your back. Dr. Keegan, give me a hand here, would you?"

Dr. Reichart billowed a sheet over Morgan as Dr. Keegan helped Morgan out of his hospital gown.

"We're going to turn you on your side, now, Morgan," Dr. Reichart said. "You can help us, okay? On three. One, two, and three."

Morgan straightened himself out like a board. The doctors couldn't turn him.

"Now, now . . . come on, Morgan. Help us out here. One, two, three."

Morgan wouldn't budge.

Dr. Reichart paused for a moment. He looked to Spaceman, who was still tending to the tank, and gestured to him for help. Spaceman came over, picked up Morgan, and flopped him over on his stomach like he was flipping a pancake.

"Thank you," said Dr. Reichart. The suit made no reply and went back to work.

"Just relax, Morgan," Dr. Keegan said. "We're not going to hurt you. Relax your shoulders."

Morgan kept himself rigid as the doctors examined his back.

"There," said Dr. Reichart. "See that ridge running down the center?"

Morgan stiffened up even more.

"Morgan, we need you to bend a little at the waist, okay? . . . Morgan? . . . *Bend.*"

Morgan wouldn't. He knew he should. His parents were probably scared. He knew he should listen to the doctors and get better. He knew in his heart that he wasn't supposed to be enjoying this. Maybe he should let the doctors fix whatever this was. If they cured him, he could go home. He could go back to the apartment— back to the city, and the traffic, and the boring Sunday afternoons, back to school, and math, and Mrs. McSwiggen.

Morgan would not bend. He was immovable.

Again Dr. Reichart gestured to Spaceman in the corner. He lurched over, reached down, and bent Morgan in half.

Actually, he only *tried* to bend Morgan in half.

Spaceman could not budge Morgan—not even a little bit. Morgan was surprised at himself. He didn't even have to try that hard. He just *thought* hard. He just quietly thought to himself:

"No."

Over and over again.

"No. I will not bend."

And he didn't.

"Forget it," ordered Dr. Reichart, pulling the sheet off Morgan. "Just put him in the pool."

Spaceman picked Morgan up and carried

him to the vat. Morgan remained as stiff as a board. Slowly he was lowered into the pool. The tank ran about ten to twelve feet across and was about four feet deep. Morgan had his back against the side of the pool and his elbows strung along the rim, holding himself up and his body straight. The water tickled his chin.

He looked down at his legs.

Through the water the glittering scales were magnified. They shimmered and sparkled as they floated just beneath the surface and gave off flashes of fluorescent greens and blues. The ashy blue-white colors of his belly and chest were deeper and brighter when wet. All the eyes up in the booth were staring in wonder.

Spaceman bent over and lifted Morgan's arms off the edge of the pool and pushed him to the middle. Morgan couldn't keep himself rigid anymore. He tried, but when he did, he just slid back and sank under the surface. He wanted to scare all of them a little, so he let himself sink to the bottom. He looked up at the hooded faces staring over the rim of the pool at him. He looked up at all the faces star-ing down from the booth wondering what was going on, and then . . .

He *finned out.*

Morgan broke though the surface of the water in full fin, and with one sweeping slap he splashed water all over the two doctors and Spaceman. Then he swam around the pool slowly and let his fin stick far out, skimming across the water like a sail.

The booth was stunned.

Pencils dropped as well as jaws. Dr. Keegan actually sat down on the floor. He just stepped back a few feet after he was splashed and sat right down on the floor. Dr. Reichart ran to a corner, papers and documents fluttering after him, and Spaceman seemed unmoved.

Morgan continued swimming in slow circles around the pool. Everything sounded so different below the surface. *Under* the water he could hear everything a thousand times more clearly, but the voices above sounded sludgy and garbled. Sort of like *they* were the ones underwater. But if Morgan concentrated, he could tune them out altogether. When he did, he heard nothing except the sound of his own movements against the water. He discovered he could stay under for a long time now without having to come up for air, and his body glided through the water as if it weren't even there. He felt enormous, and at the same time he felt like he weighed nothing. He was weightless and huge. Like a six-foot-two two-hundred-fifty-pound ballet dancer floating in outer space.

It was a wonderful feeling.

The fin was really a fin now. Morgan could move it from side to side or up and down. It felt like another hand. The thin, filmy membrane that connected the spines of the fin was now a strong leathery skin stretched tight from one spine to another. It was a brilliant deep blue, speckled with silver and black sparkles and edged in soft sea-green brush strokes. It was absolutely beautiful, and absolutely not human.

"*Makaira ampla*," Morgan said underwater to himself. "*Makaira ampla.*"

CHAPTER SEVENTEEN

THE SCALES CONTINUED TO SPREAD over Morgan's body. By the end of the first week they had spread halfway up his back. They encircled the dorsal fin (which had grown another three and a quarter inches out of his back, standing now at a full twenty-two inches), and a few were spreading down the backs of his arms. Doctors and nurses dressed in identical space suits came in hourly and took measurements of everything they could possibly measure. The size of the scales, the rate of hair loss (Morgan's hair had fallen completely out on the third night), the size of the fin, the lengths of the spikes, and the distances between them. They took pictures, scraped samples, recorded recordings, and even videotaped him finning out.

Morgan had finning out down to a science. He would dive under the water in the pool and start to circle the bottom to get up a little momentum. Whenever he did this, whoever was in the room would always come over to the edge of the pool to see where he had disappeared to. Which was just what Morgan wanted. He'd watch them lean their gawking heads over the side, chattering away. When enough people had gathered around the rim, he would kick up to the surface, and just before he broke through, he would quickly flip his fin out and violently twist his upper body in a kind of S shape. This would create a huge three-hundred-sixty-degree splash that could soak anyone who was even remotely close to the pool. Whenever he did it, he gave a bewildered look to the dripping doctors as if to say he couldn't help it.

Morgan was getting pretty used to everyone milling about the Vat Room, as he called it. All except for silent Spaceman, who was the only one allowed to take Morgan out of the pool and put him back in when they needed to do tests on him or feed him intravenously. Every time he was taken out, Morgan flopped and squiggled every which way he could. The oil in the water and the lotions they had applied to his body made him extremely hard to hold on to.

Today was another day for tests. Spaceman had just gone through fourteen lunges before he finally caught Morgan under the arms and wrestled him to the surface. Morgan wriggled and shook his bald head all the way to the examining table.

"Thank you," Dr. Reichart said to the oh-so-silent one, who flopped Morgan down on the examining table and walked away.

They had done quite a few of these examinations on Morgan, so he knew the routine, even if he didn't like it. He would lie on his side and gently spread out his fin. The doctors would then stretch it out on the examining table. Morgan thought this was probably his payback for all those moths (he couldn't find any butterflies) he had pinned to a cardboard box cover for last year's biology project.

"Another quarter inch," marveled Dr. Ashley as she measured the centermost spike. "Still growing."

Dr. Ashley spent all her time studying the fin and where it was connected along his spine. Dr. Keegan kept looking in wonder and taking notes, and Dr. Reichart was busy busy writing his paper for the medical journal. He kept a little tape recorder with him and was always talking to himself.

"Any new sensations today?" he asked one afternoon, sticking the tape recorder in front of Morgan's face.

"Ai aien awk, oo ozo." *(I can't talk, you bozo.)*

"Oh, yes . . . that's right. Here you go," he continued, handing Morgan the chalk to write on the board.

Then something extraordinary happened.

Morgan could not hold on to the chalk.

"Got the dropsies?" Dr. Reichart said, thinking he was funny, and handed Morgan the chalk again.

He dropped it again.

"What's seems to be the—" Dr. Reichart started to say. "Doctors," he said softly to the others. They all turned to look.

Morgan's thumbs were gone.

Both of them.

Well, they weren't exactly gone—they were just sort of connected to his index fingers, fused by a tiny spread of skin. So tiny that you could just barely see a little light between the two fingers. There was nothing between the index and middle finger; but the middle finger, ring finger, and pinky were fused together also. The skin connecting them was just like the skin that connected the spikes on his back.

"Now do you believe me?" Dr. Keegan said as his head popped up over Morgan's hand to get a better look.

"Webbing of the thumb and index finger on both hands . . ." Dr. Reichart whispered into his tape recorder, ignoring Dr. Keegan.

"Check his toes," Dr. Ashley said, taking over.

Dr. Keegan disappeared for a moment and then popped up at the foot of the table.

"Webbed," he said. "All of them."

"Toes as well. Webbed. Preliminary diagnosis revealed . . ." continued Dr. Reichart into his tape recorder.

Morgan held his hands up to the light and spread what was left of his fingers. The shadows they made on his bed sheet looked like claws. He tried to wiggle his toes, but they wouldn't wiggle. The whole foot just flapped.

"It's progressing at an incredible rate," Dr. Ashley said quietly to Dr. Keegan. "We need to make a decision. Soon." She gestured for Spaceman. "You can put him back."

Spaceman lifted Morgan up and carried him back to the pool. Dr. Reichart followed after, excitedly talking into his recorder.

"Clear the room, please," Dr. Ashley called

out. The rest of the assorted doctors and nurses filed out. "Everyone," she added.

The booth hesitated.

"Yes, that means you!" she yelled.

Everyone cleared out of the booth.

Morgan was swirling the water back and forth with his hands. It was like the time he went swimming at the YMCA and wore the plastic flippers on his hands instead of his feet. He finned out with a little splash and dove under the water. He swam in slow, easy circles around the pool, tuning out the conversation of the doctors.

"Over here," Dr. Ashley called to Dr. Reichart.

The three of them went to the far corner of the room and swooshed closed a curtain that hung from the ceiling.

"We need to make a decision," Dr. Ashley said with some urgency. "It's dangerously close to the spinal cord right now and growing in deeper every day."

"I don't think we should operate yet," said Dr. Keegan. "We have no idea what this is or what damage we might do if we start *removing* things."

Morgan heard the part about removing

things and decided to tune in.

"And what damage might we do if we let whatever this is overtake this poor boy's body?" Dr. Ashley asked.

"What about the journal?" asked Dr. Reichart. "Shouldn't we let it progress a little more so we can get an accurate report? The—"

"Oh, please, enough with the stupid journal," said Dr. Keegan.

"But we could get in the record books with this one," continued Dr. Reichart. "No one has ever grown a fin! A fin like this is—"

"But I've got his spinal column involved here," said Dr. Ashley. "I need to move fast."

The three doctors grew silent.

"We'll need his parents' permission," said Dr. Keegan reluctantly.

"Permission for what?" Morgan thought, breaking the surface to catch a breath.

"They haven't even seen the fin yet," Dr. Reichart mentioned. "They've been in quarantine all week."

"Well, find some suits for them and get them up here," said Dr. Ashley. "It's time they knew exactly what was going on."

CHAPTER EIGHTEEN

THE THREE DOCTORS swooshed the curtains from around them and headed out of the room. Dr. Reichart stopped by the pool on the way out.

"Morgan," he said, tapping on the side of the tank.

Morgan popped up, shaking the water from his face.

"Ai, Oc."

"Hi. You're going to get to see your parents tonight."

"Eely?"

"Yes. Try and get some rest. We'll be back later."

Morgan dove backward and backstroked across the pool. When everyone was gone, Spaceman came back in and closed the door behind him. He sat in a chair next to the door, folded his arms, and stared at Morgan. At least Morgan thought he was staring at him. The face-mask part of his suit was fogged up like everyone else's, so it was hard to tell where he was looking.

"Not polite to stare," Morgan thought at him as he swam down to the bottom of the pool and stayed there. Another change had happened to Morgan. He was now able to hold his breath for really long periods of time. It didn't even feel like holding his breath. It sort of felt like he was breathing through his body. Well, not really through his body, more like through his skin. It was an odd sensation. It was a little like the way it felt to breathe when his mom put Vicks VapoRub on his chest when he was sick. Like something cool and clean was being pulled *through* him. It would have been hard for him to describe. It felt like each pore was taking long, tight breaths of icy air.

Suddenly someone banged into the tank. Morgan looked up, and there was Spaceman. His hood looked wiggly through the water. Morgan wondered what he wanted. He never came over to the tank when there weren't any doctors around.

He just stared at Morgan.

Morgan wasn't coming up.

"Stare all you want."

Morgan lay on the bottom of the tank with his back pressed up against the side. He had to flip and flap a little bit every now and then to stay in one place. But it wasn't too hard. Morgan stared back at the wavy suit that was looking down at him.

He would have stayed there for a long time if Spaceman hadn't dropped his hood in the pool. He was leaning over the tank to try to get a better look at Morgan through the water, and his hood slipped right off his head. That's when Morgan saw that it wasn't Spaceman after all.

Morgan hurried to the surface.

"These stupid— Could you . . ." Molly said, fumbling about, "could you grab that for me, honey?"

"Ai, Ahwee!" Morgan yelled.

"Hi there," she said with a grin. "Could you—dear? Could you get that? If Dr. Reichart sees me . . ."

Morgan finned out, without a splash, and dove to the bottom to get Molly's hood. It was billowed open in the water, so he swam into it and broke through the surface with it on his head.

"You're a sweetie," she said, lifting it off his head. "Thanks." She held it up like a dirty diaper. "Things just don't stay on my head. I don't understand it." She put the wet hood back on, snapped a few snaps at the neckline, and clumsily zippered a zipper. "I don't know why they make these things so hard to get into."

Morgan waited patiently for her to finish and then swam up under her nose.

"Well, look at you, you little fish, you."

"Auwrin."

"Sorry. You little *marlin*, you," she said, correcting herself. "What happened to your hair?" she asked as she rubbed a gloved hand across his bald head.

"Ei el awf."

"By itself? Goodness. Well, it's kind of cute anyway. Oh, my . . ." she said, feeling down the back of his head. "The scales are moving up your neck."

"Ai oh. Ook!" he said, and finned out like a proud peacock. He swam around the tank and shimmied the fin back and forth to knock the water off it.

"That's beautiful," she said. "Just beautiful."

"An ook aeh ish!" he said, holding up his webbed hands and feet.

"My, oh my . . ." Molly stammered.

Morgan dove under the water to show Molly how fast he could swim. He circled the bottom of the tank as fast as he could. The water started to form a little whirlpool up on top, and Morgan broke through the surface in the center of it. He swam over to Molly.

"Um awn ein."

"I can't go in there, Morgan. I'd get fired."

"Um awwnn!"

"No. I can't," she said a little sternly. "Listen," she said in a whisper. "I'm not supposed to be here. I just wanted to say good luck before the—"

Morgan heard people outside the glass doors.

"I have to go," she said quickly. "I have to— I'll see you later."

"Eight! Och ish!" *(Wait! Watch this!)* Morgan said, and dove backward with a big splashy back flop. When he came back up, Molly was gone and Spaceman was staring at him. Morgan pushed himself off the side of the

150

tank and floated on his back in the middle of the pool.

Above him, the lights of the booth flickered on. He heard voices and the click of the microphones being turned on again.

Then he thought he heard his mother. He stopped floating and cocked his head a bit to hear better.

Yes, it was his mother.

She was in the booth.

She was talking to Dr. Ashley.

CHAPTER NINETEEN

HE GROWTH ON HIS BACK is our biggest concern at the moment," Morgan heard Dr. Ashley explain to his parents.

"What kind of growth?" asked his mother.

"Well, that's why we've asked you up here. Morgan?" she called down. "You've got some company."

Morgan saw his parents at the window in the booth. "Ai, Om! Ai, Ahd!" he yelled up.

They both leaned into the microphone at the same time.

"Hi, honey," his mom said.

"Hey there, sport," added his dad.

"It's progressed a lot since you last saw him," said Dr. Ashley.

"His hair," his mother said, a little dazed. "Morgan, what happened to your hair?"

"Ei el awf!"

"It fell out early this week," Dr. Reichart explained to her.

"What's that on his chest and his stomach?" asked his father. Morgan listened closely too. He wanted to hear what the doctor had to say.

"We don't know yet," said Dr. Ashley. "Some sort of second skin that's spread across the underside of his body."

"Those scaly things are everywhere," his father continued. "He's starting to look like a fi—"

"Yes?" said Dr. Keegan.

"Uh . . . nothing."

"You were going to say a *fish*, weren't you?"

"Well, it's just that he looks a little like a—"

"Uh auwrin!" shouted Morgan as best he could.

"What did he say?" his father asked.

"I believe he said, 'A marlin.'"

"Ash ight!"

"The growths are very similar in many characteristics to the skin of the *Makaira ampla*," Dr. Ashley explained to his parents. "The blue marlin, that is."

Morgan waited to hear what his parents would say.

They said nothing.

"We have no explanation for this phenomenon so far," Dr. Reichart offered. "The growths are progressing at a amazing rate."

153

"Why?" asked his mother. "Why is this happening?"

"I'm sorry, but at this point we have no idea. Our biggest concern right now is to stop it before it progresses too far."

"Too far?" asked his mother.

"I'm afraid, at this rate, it could prove life threatening."

"Oh my—"

Morgan heard his mother getting upset. He called up to the booth. "Ey! Om! Ey! Ai oheh! Eely! Ai eel ine!" He lunged for a plastic writing board that hung from the side of the vat and struggled to hold on to it. He slapped wildly at the pen, which hung from a little string, trying to trap it with his webbed hand. He finally caught it, clamped it between what was lift of his fingers, and scrawled out a message to his mom. He held it up.

"What's that say?" asked his mom. "I don't have my glasses."

His father read it aloud. "It says: DON'T WORRY, MOM. I'M OK!"

"Ai ine!!" Morgan yelled up and dove underwater again. That's when he noticed that he didn't blink anymore. He used to have to

154

blink a lot to keep his focus clear while he was under the water, but lately he had been needing to do this less and less. Now he didn't need to blink at all. Actually, he couldn't if he wanted to. He tried to a few times. His eyes wouldn't blink. Morgan broke the surface. He reached up and felt his eyelids with his webbed fingers. Both his eyelashes and his eyebrows were gone. His eyelids were still there, but they wouldn't work. It didn't really bother Morgan under the water, but when he popped his head up, his eyes dried up really fast.

Morgan was beginning to need to stay *under*water more than he needed to stay *out* of the water.

"Ey, Om! Och ish!" Morgan yelled up, and dove back under the water.

"What's he doing?" Morgan heard his father ask.

His hearing underwater was even stronger now. The garbled sounds that he used to hear were now clear, soft tones. Underwater, everything sounded like *easy-listening* music.

"Oh, he's just playing. He won't be up for a while," Dr. Keegan told his dad. "Just watch."

Dr. Keegan spoke into the microphone. "Two minutes, Morgan."

"Dr. Keegan," Dr. Ashley said, trying to keep the conversation on track.

"Just a moment," he answered.

"He's under a long time, isn't he?" his father asked after a few long minutes.

"Oh, he's fine," Dr. Keegan answered. He spoke into the microphone again. "*Five* minutes, Morgan."

Morgan slowly swam around the bottom of the pool. Minutes passed. He heard his father getting nervous.

"This is ridiculous. No one can—"

"Shhh," Dr. Keegan said to his dad. "I think he's going for a record."

"That's not humanly possible," said his father.

"Exactly," said Dr. Keegan. "Eight and a half minutes!"

Suddenly Morgan burst from beneath the water in full fin. He shook his head from side to side and twisted his glittering body, throwing water everywhere. He looked up to the booth with a big smile.

"He loves to do that," Dr. Keegan said to

Morgan's parents. "Eight minutes and fifty-three seconds!" he said proudly into the microphone.

"Eah ieaeh-ee!!" Morgan shouted, and flopped back into a backstroke.

"What is that!?" Morgan heard his mother ask. He looked up to see her staring at his fin. He'd forgotten that they hadn't seen it before.

"Ish ai inn!" Morgan shouted up. "Ish ai inn!"

"It's his fin," Dr. Ashley said matter-of-factly.

"A fin!?" his father asked.

"Yes, a fin. And it needs to come off."

"OT?!" Morgan yelled up.

"Nothing, Morgan," Dr. Ashley answered.

"You mean . . . an operation?" asked his mother.

"Yes," Dr. Ashley said bluntly.

"Eight uh innu! Ai owe oo ai eel ine!" *(Wait a minute! I told you I feel fine!)*

"Just a minute, honey," his mom said. "When would you do it?" she continued to Dr. Ashley.

"Tomorrow morning. As early as possible."

"Is there any . . . any risk?"

"Yes, there is."

"Well . . ." Mom said, "well, we need to talk about this."

"Of course," Dr. Ashley said, assuring her.

"OM!" Morgan shouted again.

"In a minute, hon. Can we go down and see him?" his mother asked.

"The room is sealed. No one is allowed in. You'll have to say good-bye from up here."

"Morgan?" his mom said into the microphone.

"Ot!?"

"We have to go now, honey. Visiting time is over."

"We'll see you tomorrow, kiddo," his father added.

"Ai eel ine! Eesh ouwn ei emm ache ai inn!" *(I feel fine! Please don't let them take my fin!)* Morgan shouted up.

"I can't understand him at all now," his mom said. "It doesn't even look like him."

Morgan's mother almost never cried, but she was crying now. His dad put an arm around her shoulders and pulled her against him.

"I think it would be best for you to go now," Dr. Ashley said. "Morgan's getting a little anxious."

"Eight!" *(Wait!)* Morgan screamed. "Eight!"

"It's best that we don't upset him anymore,"

Dr. Ashley continued, escorting his parents out of the booth. "He needs his rest."

"AHD! AHD!!"

MORGAN DIDN'T NEED MUCH SLEEP anymore. At night he'd swim in long, gentle circles around the pool just below the surface. His arms and webbed hands trailed along his sides, and his bald head quietly pushed little ripples of water in front of him. Every ten or twelve minutes he would roll over on his side and take a breath and then softly roll back down.

That was what sleeping was like for him now.

He could even dream with his eyes open. When the lights in the room went out at night, the water turned pitch-black. His dreams happened in the dark waters. They floated out in front of him.

It was late.

Morgan had been swim-sleeping off and on for about an hour. The room was dark except for the green and red pin lights of monitors and machines that flashed around the room like Christmas decorations. They reflected off the glassy water in Morgan's tank. Some of the reflections caught his scales when he swam into them and shot off colored blossoms of fluorescent sparkles that danced and flittered along the ceiling.

The booth was darkened.

The room was empty.

And quiet.

No one was around.

Except the shadow that moved in the corner.

Morgan flung his head out of the water and spun around in circles, looking all about the room. He peered up toward the booth, over to the door, and around the length of the room. It was too dark to see anything, but something was different. He could feel that something was different.

There was someone in the room.

He folded his fin in and slunk up to the back of the tank. He dunked his head underwater for an instant because his eyes were stinging. When he popped back up, the shadow had moved a little closer.

Morgan was scared.

Whoever this was, wasn't supposed to be in the room this late, in the dark, with nobody else around. Morgan didn't know what to do. So he did what any fish would do. He dove to the bottom and stayed there. The figure came up to the edge and stared down at Morgan. Morgan made himself as small as he could. He felt like a fish in a barrel.

He was.

The shadowy figure stayed in one spot and stared down at Morgan.

Morgan stared back up.

The figure waited.

Five minutes, eight, ten, twelve . . . Morgan was scared, so it was harder for him to stay under this long. His heart was pounding . . . fourteen minutes . . . the figure wouldn't move . . .

"Just go away," Morgan thought over and over to himself.

Fifteen and half minutes. Morgan had never stayed under that long before.

Finally, at seventeen minutes and six seconds, Morgan could stay under no longer. He burst up through the surface, gasping and clutching at breaths.

"Ot ou oo awnt!?" *(What do you want!?)*

he yelled at the figure.

"Shhh," the shadow said.

"Ai'll scheem!" *(I'll scream!)* Morgan screamed.

"No one can hear you," it replied.

The figure stepped a little closer to Morgan. Morgan scooted farther around the tank to keep his distance. The figure reached out its arm and turned on a small light that was next to the tank.

Then the figure stepped into the light. It was wearing an overcoat cinched up tight around its neck, an old baseball cap, and sunglasses.

The figure stepped back a little bit into the light and took off its sunglasses, and Morgan could see its eyes, its brilliant blue-black eyes.

"Hello, Morgan," it said in a gravelly deep voice.

It was the old marlin.

The same one he had seen on the sidewalk in front of his building.

"Do you remember me?"

Morgan slowly nodded his head yes.

"Meet some friends of mine."

From the shadows behind the old marlin a

small crowd of men stepped forward. All of them had on overcoats, hats, and sunglasses. They kept their hands in their pockets and huddled about the old marlin, gently nudging shoulders to try to get a better look at Morgan.

"It's a school," Morgan thought. "A whole school of Marlin men!"

They stared at Morgan with twinkling eyes and wondering faces. They were wearing hats of every shape and size: wool caps; old fedoras; a crushed, faded straw cowboy hat; a few baseball caps; and some hats that Morgan had never seen before. All the Marlins stood there with their brims pulled low on their foreheads and slouched about their ears. Their sunglasses were all different shapes too. Some were square, some were round, some were little rectangles, and others wrapped around eyes like fancy race-car-driver glasses. All their overcoats were buttoned up to their necks and cinched up tight around their ears.

They all looked different.

They all looked the same.

"This gets weirder all the time," Morgan thought to himself.

Some were in the light more than others,

but Morgan could make out most of their faces. They themselves were all different shapes and sizes too. Some were small and heavy, some were tall. Some were white men and some were black men. Some were old, and some were not so old. Once they settled in around the old Marlin, they too, took off their sunglasses, in unison. They all took off their hats. Every head shimmered bald in the little bit of light that filtered through the room.

Their eyes were Marlin eyes.

"Hello, Morgan," they said in unison.

They did everything in unison. But it wasn't like they *tried* to do it, they just . . . did, like a flock of birds that suddenly turns in one direction. Thousands of birds make the same turn at the same time, and you wonder: Who turned first? But no one turns first, they just *know*.

"Ai," Morgan said warily.

"We've been waiting to meet you," the school thought out in unison.

Morgan noticed something else. When they spoke, nobody moved his lips. It didn't even sound like their voices were coming from the direction of their mouths. The sound just sort of came *out* of them, out of the centers of their bodies or something.

"I can hear what they're thinking!" Morgan thought to himself.

"We can hear you, too," the old Marlin said, with only a smile moving on his lips. "We've been listening to you for a long time. We all heard you."

"Ahn ai ou aht?" *(Can I do that?)* Morgan asked.

"Stop trying to use your voice. Just *think* to me what you want to say."

Morgan concentrated for a moment, furrowed his brows, and thought hard in the direction of the old Marlin. The old men behind him waited for an expectant moment, and then they all gently shook their heads from side to side.

"Don't try so hard," the old Marlin thought at Morgan.

"This is crazy," Morgan thought to himself.

"There you go," the old Marlin thought back. "That was easy, wasn't it?"

"You? You heard that?"

The crowd behind nodded their heads in synchronized approval.

"Well, we don't really *hear*, but yes, I

understood you."

"Cool."

"Yes. Cool," thought the school.

"And we can just talk to each other like this? All the time?" Morgan asked.

"Well, it's not really *talking* either. But yes, this is how we communicate. We call it *understanding* one another."

"But who *are* you guys?" Morgan asked. "Why is this happening to me?"

"I'll tell you more about that later, when you're released."

"Released?" Morgan thought to him.

"Yes. That's why we're here," thought the old Marlin.

"That's why we're here," echoed the school.

"They're letting me go?" Morgan thought. "No one said anything to me. My—"

"No one's letting you go, Morgan," thought the old Marlin. "We've come to take you."

"Where?"

"Home," thought the school.

"I can't go home like this," thought Morgan to them. "I only have a little bathtub. I'll drown in there."

"You're going home, Morgan," thought the

old Marlin. "But not to where you think."

"We're running out of time," thought one of the Marlins from behind.

"They'll be here soon," thought another.

"Morgan," the old Marlin thought, "there are some people coming for you tonight."

"So?"

"You're scheduled for an operation to-morrow."

"I know."

"To remove your fin. To remove what makes you a Marlin."

Morgan stopped for a moment when he heard the old Marlin say this. It was the first time anyone had actually called him a Marlin. He considered what the old Marlin had said for a short while and then, very softly, very seriously, he asked:

"I am a Marlin, aren't I?"

The old Marlin nodded his head with a smile, "Yes. You are."

"And they want to take that away."

"Yes, they do."

Morgan considered this and then looked up at the old Marlin. "How did you find me?"

"Well, you have a little friend around here

who's been watching you and telling us everything that's been going on. You'll understand more about that later. Right now we don't have much time. There's somebody coming to sedate you very soon, and we have to get you out of here before he shows up."

"I don't know . . . I think I should ask my parents first. I'll get grounded for sure if—"

"Morgan," the old Marlin broke in. "These people will take away everything that makes you a Marlin if you stay here. It happened to us. And many others like us. You musn't believe what they tell you. It's up to you. Do you want us to get you out of here?"

Morgan thought for a moment. He was staring at about a dozen or so pretty strange-looking bald men who wanted to kidnap him from the hospital. He wondered who in his right mind would go anywhere with these guys.

"I would," he thought to himself. "Let's go."

"Yes," thought the school as they put their hats and glasses back on.

"Where are we gonna go?"

"You'll see."

"But . . . my mother—shouldn't we leave a

note or something?"

"I'll take care of everything," the old Marlin thought, assuring Morgan. "Trust me." He turned to the other Marlins behind him and thought, "Let's go."

The school circled around the tank. One of them pulled an old overcoat out of a bag he carried and stepped toward Morgan.

"Help us out here," thought one of the Marlins, as he tried to put the coat over Morgan's scaly arms and webbed hands. "There you go," he continued as he buttoned it up around Morgan's neck. Morgan was standing in the tank. "Now duck under and get all of it wet. It's got to last awhile."

Morgan ducked under the water with the overcoat on. It clung to him as he stood up again.

"Hat!" the same Marlin thought to the school around him. A baseball cap came around the tank, passed along from hand to hand like a hot dog at a ball game.

"Same thing with the hat," thought the Marlin to Morgan as he tossed the baseball cap to him. Morgan tried to catch it, but it fell between his webbed hands. He grabbed at it again and slopped it onto his bald head. It was too big for him and sat way down over his ears and eyes. The Marlins all laughed a little laugh.

"Glasses," another Marlin thought, and passed a pair of sunglasses around from Marlin to Marlin. "Try these."

Morgan did, and looked up for approval.

"Okay, okay, this isn't a fashion show," the old Marlin said. "We need to get going."

"Take another dunk, Morgan," thought one of the Marlins. "It's a long drive. You've got to keep yourself wet."

Morgan dove back under with his baseball cap, overcoat, and sunglasses on and took one more look at his stainless-steel tank. Then he splashed back up, and two of the Marlins reached in and took hold of him. They handed him to the Marlin who was wearing the old straw cowboy hat.

"I'm getting too old for this," he thought to Morgan as he cradled him in his arms. He had a face that was creviced like weatherworn folds of leather, but his blue-blue eyes smiled and danced. He carried Morgan to the glass door.

"Someone's coming," Morgan suddenly thought.

"What?" thought the old Marlin.

"Can't you hear it? Someone's coming. Listen." They all stood very still and listened.

"He's right. Someone's coming!" the old Marlin thought-cried. "Put him back in!"

The school scattered.

The cowboy Marlin spun around and tossed Morgan back into the tank. Someone flicked the light off, and everyone retreated into the shadows of the room.

"Stay under," the old Marlin thought to Morgan from the shadows.

Morgan took off his sunglasses and slunk under. He could hear whoever it was coming through the doors of the gymnasium. Before he was halfway across the room, Morgan knew who it was from the sound of his steps.

Spaceman.

Through the rippled surface of his water, Morgan could see the glass door open. Spaceman came in. He was carrying something in his hands. He paused by the open door, looking as if he had noticed something different in the room. Then he shut the door and headed over to the tank. He stood staring at Morgan.

Then Morgan felt someone coming forward from the shadows behind him. No, he felt all of them coming forward. The whole school of Marlins were coming forward to face off with oh-so-silent, helmet-head Spaceman. Morgan swam to the far end of the tank and floated up so that just the crown of his hat and his eyes were sitting on the top of the water. He drifted there like a lily pad.

Suddenly the lights flashed on and Spaceman was face-to-face with a whole school of sunglass-wearing, not-to-be-messed-with Marlins.

The old Marlin stepped forward. He slowly took off his sunglasses and thought toward Spaceman, "Where have you been? We were going to leave without you."

Spaceman thought back, "There are doctors everywhere down there. I couldn't get past them." He pulled off the hood of his space suit and glanced over at Morgan.

Spaceman had Marlin eyes.

"We're going to have to go down the back fire stairs," he continued.

"Did you bring the saline?"

"Right here," thought Spaceman, pulling

173

out a little spritzer bottle of water from his coat.

"Good," thought the old Marlin. "Make sure you keep him wet," he continued to the other Marlins. "Morgan, come on over here."

Morgan slowly sidled up on the side of the tank near the old Marlin.

"I believe you two have met," he thought to Morgan as he gestured across the pool.

"Hello, Morgan," thought Spaceman as he stepped out of his suit.

"Hi," Morgan shyly thought back.

Spaceman smiled, and then someone from the crowd tossed him an overcoat. He put it on and pulled out a pair of mirrored sunglasses from one of the pockets. Out of the other pocket he took an old wool cap and rolled it down over his bald head. He buttoned and cinched up his coat and said, "Let's go. They'll be here any minute."

Spaceman Marlin leaned over and easily scooped Morgan up in his arms. "Better put those back on," he said, gesturing to Morgan's sunglasses. Morgan fumbled with the glasses in his webbed hands. "Here. Let me," Spaceman said, taking them. As Spaceman was wiping them dry against his coat, Morgan looked up and saw his own face reflected in the mirrored glasses that Spaceman was wearing.

Morgan had to stare.

It was the first time he had seen his own eyes.

They were Marlin eyes.

CHAPTER TWENTY-ONE

ABOUT A HALF DOZEN of the Marlins started out of the vat room first and peered through the swinging doors that led to the gymnasium. When they signaled that the coast was clear, Spaceman carried Morgan out into the hall.

Once outside, the rest of the Marlins formed a tight circle around Morgan and Spaceman.

"Come on," came a thought from the Marlin by the door.

They all moved as one. They walked in step together. They stopped together to look around. The swing of their arms, the turn of their heads, and even the unconscious adjusting of hat brims were all done in perfect, unplanned unison.

Spaceman didn't say anything. He stayed in the middle of the school of Marlins holding Morgan in his arms.

"You're not much of a gabber, are you?" Morgan thought up to Spaceman as he carried him along.

"Shhh" was all he thought back.

Morgan wondered why he should be shushed if no one but other Marlins could hear him. It didn't make sense.

"We need to think, that's why."

They made their way across the gymnasium, and a few Marlins ran ahead to peer out the swinging doors on the opposite side.

"All clear," a Marlin thought back.

They went through the swinging doors and turned to the right. Morgan could see that they were headed toward another set of doors that had a red-lettered EXIT sign above them. They went through these and headed down the stairs. As they made their way down, a nurse suddenly came bustling through a door.

"Ook ou!" *(Look out!)* Morgan yelled, but it was too late.

The nurse went barreling into the Marlins surrounding Morgan. She dropped a tray of pills that she was carrying, and they waterfalled down the steps.

"I'd drop my head if it weren't on my

shoulders," the nurse said apologetically as she gathered up the pills. "I'm so sorry . . . I— excuse me—"

"Ahwee!" *(Molly!)* Morgan cried from Spaceman's arms.

"Quiet," thought the old Marlin.

"Ish oheh, ish ohwee Ahwee!" Morgan said. "I mean, it's okay, it's only Molly," he then thought to the Marlin. "She's my friend."

"Morgan? Is that you?" Molly said. "Is that you?"

"Up, ish ee!" *(Yup, it's me!)*

"Why, look at you, you little—" Suddenly Molly's face changed. She stood up, straightened her dress, tore off her cap, which wobbled on the side of her head, and walked up to Spaceman.

"What on earth do think you're doing with that boy! You put him back this instant!"

"Ahwee, eire ohwee—" *(Molly, they're only—)*

"Now! Do you hear me?! I don't know who you are or what— Don't you touch me! Don't you touch me!" she screamed at one of the Marlins, who made a step toward her. "What's going on here!?"

Most of the Marlins looked a little bit like

scolded schoolboys. They dropped their heads down and shuffled their feet in unison.

"Is somebody in charge here!?" Molly continued. "Well, come on . . . speak up!"

Everyone looked to the old Marlin.

"Ee ish," Morgan said.

The old Marlin came forward and thought at Molly. "Molly," he thought.

Molly spun around. "Who said that!?"

"She can hear us?" Morgan laughed up to the old Marlin.

"She can hear *me*," thought the old Marlin as he stepped down to Molly. "It'll take some practice before *you* can understand non-Marlins," he continued as he passed by and got closer to Molly. She backed up a step.

"It was me, Molly," thought the old Marlin. "I'm in charge."

Molly stared at him for a moment as he talked—or rather, as he thought.

"What are you, a ventriloquist?" she finally said. "You think this is some kind of joke? This is a sick boy. He—"

"Molly, calm down. We're not here to harm Morgan. We—"

"You're darn tootin' you're not! You—"

"MOLLY!" the old Marlin yelled at her. "Don't make me yell. Please."

"Ish aw ight, Ahwee" (*It's all right, Molly*), Morgan tried to tell her.

"Molly, this is no joke," the old Marlin thought to her. "We've come to take Morgan where he'll be safe."

"Who's *we*?" asked Molly.

The old Marlin waited for a moment, and then he thought to the school, "Show her."

Molly turned to look at the Marlins behind her. They took their overcoats off. Some of them opened their shirts to the waist, and others rolled up their sleeves.

Morgan couldn't believe his eyes, and from the way Molly looked at him, neither could she. The leathery ash-white skin that had been seen before only on Morgan was peeking through their open shirts. The arms of others were covered in scales. They were a much darker gray-blue than Morgan's, but they were definitely scales.

Molly turned back to face the old Marlin.

"*That* is we," he thought to her.

Molly looked at the group surrounding Morgan. The school and Morgan, in unison, took off their sunglasses and looked at Molly with their huge, electric-blue–black eyes. Then they all nodded at the same time in affirmation of what the old Marlin had said. Morgan didn't know how he knew to do everything in unison with them, he just did.

"Well, my goodness" was all she could say.

"Eire oheh, Ahwee," Morgan said to her. "Eire ush aik ee!" *(They're just like me!)*

"We could have been," the old Marlin whisper-thought, then he spoke to Molly again. "Now listen, there are people coming to hurt Morgan."

"Who!?" she demanded to know.

"The doctors."

"Well, I know they're coming. There's an operation scheduled for this morning," she said. "But they won't hurt him. They—"

"Eh onna ache ai inn" (*They want to take my fin*), Morgan said to her.

"They what?" she asked.

"His fin," thought the old Marlin. "The operation is to take away his fin."

"Well, he can't very well go through life with a dorsal fin sticking out his back, now can he?"

"Ai ot?" (*Why not?*) Morgan asked.

The old Marlin stepped in between them. "Molly," he thought softly to her, "Morgan is no longer a boy with a little *Marlin* in him. He is a Marlin with a little *boy* in him. He can't go back."

Molly looked at Morgan. Morgan smiled at her and nodded his head yes.

"Ai onna oh, Ahwee." *(I want to go, Molly.)*

She thought for a moment. "Well, where are you going to take him?" she finally asked.

The old Marlin paused for a second before he answered.

"To the sea."

CHAPTER TWENTY-TWO

MOLLY WAS THE LOOKOUT NOW.

At the bottom of the stairs was an emergency exit into the back parking lot. They were all just about to bustle out the back door when Morgan thought to them, "If we go out there the alarm will go off." He pointed up to a big lettered warning that said just that.

Molly peeked through the door that led to the first floor of the hospital.

"It's too crowded in there," she said after turning back. "They'll spot you for sure. Where's your car?"

"Right out back," thought the old Marlin.

"Great. You just go for it, and I'll stay here in the stairway. When someone comes to check the alarm, I'll say it was me. I'm always doing stupid things like that anyway. They're sure to believe me."

"Ash uh ood iear, Ahwee," (*That's a good*

183

idea, Molly), Morgan said.

"You'll have to move fast, though," said Molly. "There's a security guard right across the hall from this door."

The old Marlin agreed to Molly's plan.

Morgan called the old Marlin over to him and thought-whispered in his ear.

The old Marlin said back to him, "I don't think that's a good idea."

Morgan whispered again. The old Marlin thought for a second. Then he scribbled something down on a piece of paper and handed it to Molly.

"Molly," he thought to her, "I'm trusting you to keep this a secret, okay?"

"What?"

"This is where we're taking Morgan tonight. We'll be moving him again in a few days. Do you think you could explain to his parents what's going on without letting the doctors find out?"

"I don't know. . . ."

"Eesh, Ahwee?" *(Please, Molly?)*

"You're gonna get me fired."

"Eesh?"

"All right," she said, giving in.

"Only his parents, Molly. Please?"

184

"All right," she said. "I can do this."

"Good," thought the old Marlin.

He turned to the rest of the Marlins, who had been arguing among themselves all this time about who would sit where in the car.

"I'm not sitting back there again. I couldn't breathe."

"Me either. Why didn't you get us a van like we told you?"

"A station wagon was the biggest thing they had!"

"Enough!" the old Marlin yelled, raising his thoughts. "You're acting like a bunch of minnows! You five go in the back with Morgan. You . . . one, two, three . . . and four, in the back *seat*. And the rest up front with me. Got it!?"

They all nodded.

"Okay." The old Marlin turned to Morgan. "Ready?"

"Yes," he thought back.

"Just a minute," Molly said, peeking out the door and into the hallway. "I'll say *when*. We have to wait till the security guard is at the far end of the hall."

The Marlins lined up waiting to break out the back door. They pulled their hats down tighter on their heads and bent a little at the knees.

"Ahwee," Morgan whispered.

Molly looked over her shoulder from the crack in the door.

"Ank oo." *(Thank you.)*

She smiled and turned back. "Go!"

"Ai, Awee!" *('Bye, Molly!)*

Out the back door they all rushed! Off went the fire alarm, and into the car went all the Marlins!

Sort of.

The back gate to the station wagon wouldn't open, so rather than waste time, Spaceman tried to push Morgan through its window.

"It's not open!" Morgan thought-yelled at Spaceman. "The window's closed!"

"Open the window!" Spaceman thought to the old Marlin, who jumped into the front seat and started the car so he could put down the electric window. When it was halfway down, Spaceman rolled Morgan in with a *falump*. Five of the other Marlins crawled in the same window. Morgan tried to scamper out of their way as they fell and *falumped* through too, but they wound up on top of one another. When Morgan tried to crawl out from under the

186

pile-up, his fin flew out.

"OW!" one of the Marlins cried as he was stuck with one of Morgan's spikes. "Put that thing away!"

"I can't!"

"He's finned out!" someone yelled.

"I can't close it!" Morgan was yelling. The spikes were pushing through his overcoat. "It's stuck on something!"

One of the Marlins unsnagged Morgan's fin and helped fold it up. Then Spaceman ran to the front passenger seat and hopped in. Morgan twisted around and peered out the window at Molly. She was giggling and acting very apologetic to two security guards who had rushed over to the stairwell. She snuck a wave out the emergency door before she closed it.

There were twelve Marlins, and Morgan made thirteen, and they were all scrunched into the old station wagon as it pulled slowly across the parking lot. A few feet were sticking out the back window, a few arms out the side ones, but everyone was in.

The car sputtered and choked along through the yellow-white shafts of streetlamp light that spotted the parking lot, and disappeared into the night.

CHAPTER TWENTY-THREE

MORGAN GAZED OUT at the night lights of the city through the back window of the old wagon. The lit windows in the skyscrapers and apartment buildings twinkled on and off like a sea of trapped stars signaling for help. Even in the dark hours of the early morning, trucks groaned, taxis sped, police sirens screamed, and millions of people began their commute to wherever they commute to in the city.

Morgan watched the traffic as they bumped and squeezed their way out of the city. In their wake, honking and screeching taxis darted in and out like sharks scavenging for food. Old shells of stranded cars with their insides torn out littered the sides of the road. Their doors were flung open, hoods flapped up, and tire-less frames bellied out on the pavement. It was a horrible mess of headlights and taillights, stopping and going, fumes and noise.

Morgan looked around and noticed that the other Marlins had all become very quiet and very still. It looked like they were all listening very intently to something.

"What are you all listening to?" Morgan asked them.

A collective thought came back: "The sea."

"I don't hear anything," he thought.

"You will," thought the old Marlin softly. "With time."

Morgan wanted to be able to hear it *now*. He screwed up his face and listened with every ounce of strength he had. The old Marlin smiled softly in the rearview mirror.

"You won't hear anything by listening *harder*, Morgan," he thought. "Don't try to *hear* the ocean, just try *not* to hear all the other noise. When you can do that, the sound of the sea will be the only thing left."

Morgan tried, but all he could hear was the noise. Every so often he squirted himself down with the spritzer bottle of water that Spaceman had given him.

"Are we there yet?" he asked after a while. They seemed to have been driving forever.

"You'll know when we're there," the old Marlin thought back.

Morgan pushed his big baseball cap up above his eyes, slumped over on a sleeping Marlin next to him, and stared out the window while the hours passed.

Finally, the traffic started to fall away, left behind with the city. Things became quieter. They drove another hour on the expressway heading east, turned onto a parkway going south for a long while, and then turned east again. Now things really started to change.

There were no cars at all on the road. And there were no more buildings, only trees.

The sun was just starting to peek up from behind the graying horizon. Morgan stared in wonder as the morning sun snuck up in the right-hand corner of the front windshield. A few stars still lingered in the darker sky above.

Morgan had never really seen a sunrise before. Of course, he had seen the sun come up in the city, but by the time it rose over the buildings in his neighborhood, it usually wasn't morning anymore.

He had never seen a dawn.

Morgan stared out the window with all his

might. A thin bump of light began to peer over the edge of the world. It snuck up a little more, and as it did, it blazed into a warm golden-yellow that puddled out in front of it like spilled paint. It skipped and splattered across the dark, silvery blue of something else that Morgan had never seen before. He looked harder.

It was the ocean.

Morgan didn't know what to say. He pushed himself up a little higher and pressed his nose against the side window. He couldn't look hard enough. Morgan glanced up to the front seat and saw the old Marlin watching him in the rearview mirror. He was smiling. So was Spaceman, who had turned around in his seat to watch Morgan.

"That's your new home," thought the old Marlin into the mirror.

Morgan could contain himself no longer. He started whacking all the sleeping Marlins around him. He took the spritzer bottle of water and started squirting all the sleeping Marlins.

"Come on, guys, wake up! (*SQUIRT!*) Check it out! (*SQUIRT!*) Look!"

Slowly the Marlins grumbled their way awake, took off their glasses, and dreamily looked out the window.

"Check it (*SQUIRT!*) out!" Morgan thought again.

They all watched with their still-sleepy eyes as the ocean raced past. They squeezed and jockeyed for position to get a better look, their faces nudging into one another.

"What's that!?" Morgan asked as some white, hilly-looking things whizzed by.

"Sand dunes," thought the old Marlin.

"They look like white mountains!" Morgan thought. "Look at them!" Past the dunes was a long stretch of white sand that ran down to meet the ocean. "Look at the waves!" Morgan thought excitedly to the Marlins nestled around him.

Great, tumbling white waves roared and crashed down against the beach, turning the sand at the shoreline dark with wet. The sound was absolutely glorious. Morgan had never heard such sounds before. He watched in wonder as wave after wave slammed against the shore in a burst of white foam, rushing itself up the beach like it was running away from the sea. After each wave crashed into the shore, it would race up the beach as far as it could, then *push* itself up, trying to put as much distance as possible between itself and the roaring sea behind it. Then it would start to lose its strength and begin falling back, as if the ocean were tugging at it, dragging it back to where it belonged, until a new wave would *slam* down on top, and the ocean could swallow the first up again.

"Can we stop?" Morgan thought to the old Marlin. "Let's stop! Let's—"

"Not just yet," he said. "You're not quite ready for the ocean."

"Well, then where are you taking me?" Morgan asked.

"Where a little fry like you can grow up some," he thought. "To the bay."

CHAPTER TWENTY-FOUR

THE ROAD THEY WERE DRIVING ON was built on a thin strip of land that divided the ocean from the bay. To his left, Morgan could see the bay brightening under the morning sun. There were no dunes on the bay side. As far as Morgan could see there were miles of marshy islands with dark blue waters snaking in and out among them.

"Looks like a big jigsaw puzzle," he thought.

Small black birds with slashes of red stripes across their wings flittered out of the short bushes that dotted the grassy banks. Seagulls searched the muddy shoals for breakfast and screamed at the sun as it rose still higher in the sky. Morgan had seen seagulls scavenging around at the garbage dumps in the city, but never had he seen them look so beautiful.

The station wagon pulled off the road and onto a small dirt driveway that led down to a locked gate.

"Are we stopping?" Morgan asked.

Spaceman jumped out of the front door and tried to open the gate. He ran around to the back of the wagon and reached inside.

"Move your feet," he thought as he reached under a sleep-rumpled Marlin.

He pulled out a tire iron and headed back to the fence. He snapped the lock clean off with one twist of the iron, and then swung open the long gate.

Beyond the gate was a parking lot. Morgan could tell that it hadn't been used in a long time. There were only faint traces of faded yellow lines that had once marked the spots for cars to park in. Everywhere, little patches of marsh grass sprouted through sun-baked cracks. Morgan peered out the window. Littered across the gray concrete were thousands of broken seashells bleached white by the sun. The car scrunched and crackled as it drove slowly over them.

"Where'd all the shells come from?" Morgan asked, face pressed to the window.

"Gulls," the old Marlin thought back as he swung the car toward the water. "That's how they eat. They grab a clam or a scallop in their beaks, fly up as high as they can, and then drop it. Cracks 'em open like peanuts."

Now they were driving alongside an old pier. Morgan could see a long stretch of pilings sticking out of the water. They looked like half-sunk telephone poles leaning in all different directions. Loops of rotted hemp line hung from some of the pilings, and still others were cracked and splintered with huge tangled balls of fishing line wrapped around them.

The old Marlin drove to the end of the pier. "Better get him into the water," he thought to everyone as he and Spaceman got out of the car. "We're going to check out a few things."

The other Marlins creaked and groaned and shook out their stiff joints, stretched their arms, and yawned their yawns as they piled themselves out of the wagon.

"Excuse me."

"Sorry."

"That's my foot, thank you, that's my foot!"

"Well, move already!"

Once out of the car, they schooled up behind the wagon, adjusted their sunglasses, pulled their hats on tight, and looked at Morgan.

"Are we going into the water?" Morgan thought anxiously.

"In a moment," thought the school while they straightened out their sleep-wrinkled overcoats.

"We'll be right back," cowboy hat thought. And with that they put their hands in their pockets, turned at the same time, and walked away.

"Hey!" Morgan thought to them. "Hey, guys! What about me?"

They kept walking.

"They'll be right back," Spaceman thought over from the pier. "Just sit tight."

"I have to stretch my fin!"

"In a moment. Stay where you are for now.'"

Morgan watched as the Marlins all shuffled away across the parking lot. They walked in unison without thinking to one another. The seashells in the parking lot scrunched quietly under their feet.

"Where are they going?" Morgan thought to the old Marlin and Spaceman, who stood on the pier.

"Just down to the water. They'll be right back."

As they neared the edge of the parking lot, the other Marlins took their hands out of their pockets and stepped out onto the marsh, squishing their way to the edge of the water-line.

"They going for a swim?" Morgan asked Spaceman.

"No."

The Marlins were all standing at the water-line. Then, in unison, they knelt down and gently touched the water. All ten of them were kneeling shoulder to shoulder. Then they sat back on their heels and stared out over the bay. They stayed there for a short moment and then, all at once, they headed back toward the car, their knees circled dark from kneeling in the wet marsh grass.

Morgan looked over and saw that the old Marlin and Spaceman were busy rigging up something off the side of the pier.

"What was that all about?" Morgan thought to Spaceman.

"They were just remembering," Spaceman thought back.

"Remembering what?" Morgan asked.

"What it was like when they were like you."

"Like me? They were like me?"

"We all were."

"Well, what happened?"

Spaceman looked at the old Marlin as if they were about to tell Morgan something important. He started to think something to Morgan, but just then the other Marlins crowded around the back of the car.

"Okay, your turn," thought the red-baseball-capped Marlin with a crinkled old grin.

"Yup, time for a swim," thought cowboy hat, leaning into the station wagon.

"Do any of you guys have names?" Morgan thought at them all.

The Marlins looked at one another with questioning smiles.

"Names?" thought back the fedora.

"No, we don't use them anymore," answered the raggedy cowboy hat.

"We don't need them," added the wide-brimmed blue-and-white cap.

"Well, how do you know who you're talking to?" Morgan asked.

The old black-wool-capped Marlin peered in. "You've been doing it since you met us. Haven't you noticed? Whenever you think to one of us, that one hears you, doesn't he?"

"Well, yeah . . . I just—" Morgan thought.

"We don't use names," continued the wool cap. "We are all Marlins."

"Come on now, you're drying up," thought the red-capped Marlin as he tried to help Morgan out of the car.

Morgan went to crawl toward them, but he couldn't.

"What are you waiting for?" asked cowboy hat.

"I think my legs are asleep," Morgan thought to them.

"Well, give them a whack or something."

Morgan threw back the folds of his trench coat to do just that—and stared down at the spot where his legs used to be.

"My legs are gone!" he thought in a yell. "They're gone!"

His legs had fused together during the night.

The Marlins all gasped in unison.

Morgan leaned back on his finny hands and stared down at what used to be his legs. It didn't even look like his two legs had become stuck together. It looked more like one *big* leg. Down the center now ran the same gray-white leathery skin that was on Morgan's chest and belly.

It ran clear down from below his chin, across his chest, over his thighs and knees, down the tops of his calves, and faded off into his webbed feet.

His feet weren't really feet anymore. They, too, had fused into each other, and the bones in his toes had grown long and thin. The gauze-thin membrane that stretched out tight between them fanned out like a webbed garden rake. Morgan couldn't believe it. He had a—

"I have a tail."

He had a tail.

There was silence, and then Spaceman thought, "He's really going to make it, isn't he?"

"Yes," answered the old Marlin. "I believe he is." Then he turned and went back to giving orders. "Let's get him into the water. Some of you keep a lookout by the gate."

Four hats took off to watch the gate. Everyone else schooled up at the edge of the pier.

"I've got you," Spaceman thought as he reached in and took Morgan out of the car. "You ready to go for a dip?"

"Let's go!" Morgan answered.

Spaceman walked toward the water. And didn't stop. He walked right off the edge of the pier and into the bay.

Morgan gasped and shuddered, flip-flapped, and kicked a bit. His hat fell over his eyes and his sunglasses were hanging from one ear. The Marlins watching laughed and cheered a little bit as Morgan flailed about. Spaceman still held him in his arms.

"It's pretty shallow here," thought Spaceman, chest deep in the water. "How's it feel?"

"Wet!" Morgan laughed as he shivered and splashed and wiggled in Spaceman's arms. "And salty. It's salty! Taste!" he thought as he splashed Spaceman. "It tastes just like salt!"

"That's no bathtub, is it?" thought the cowboy hat.

"No sir!" Morgan laughed again. "Come on in!!"

"Whoa, there," said Spaceman as he dunked Morgan completely under the water. He stayed down there with him for a while. It was pretty dark under the water. It had gotten muddied up when they had jumped from the pier. Billowy clouds of brown water dust floated in front of their faces. Morgan flailed his webbed hands around trying to find Spaceman's face.

"I can't see anything!"

"The bay's muddier than the ocean," Spaceman thought to him. "Just stay still for a second and it'll settle down."

"I want to fin out! Can I fin out!?"

"Sure," thought Spaceman. "Let's get this stuff off first."

Morgan swam to the surface, and Spaceman helped him off with his overcoat and tossed it up onto the pier. Then he turned Morgan over in his arms so his belly was facing down. He held him there, the way grown-ups hold kids when they're teaching them to swim for the first time. Morgan remembered that feeling, the feeling of being held, the way his father used to hold him a long time ago when he would fly him through the air like Superman.

Spaceman lowered him in the water a bit.

"Well, go ahead," he thought to Morgan.

Morgan shot his fin out.

It swooshed up through the water and splashed through the surface. Spaceman lowered Morgan a little more, dunking him underwater, and then lifted him up again. Every time he was lowered, Morgan closed up his fin, and every time he came up, he shot it back out again. Then he tried out his new tail. On the way down he slapped his tail on the water with a loud *FALAP* to see how big a splash he could make. Water flew in all directions. Morgan looked up at the pier and saw all the Marlins watching him.

He tried to splash them.

FALAP!

"Come on in!" Morgan laughed and squealed and did it again.

FALAP!!

The Marlins all looked over toward the old Marlin, who was leaning against the station wagon with folded arms. Morgan looked at him too.

"What?" the old Marlin asked of the school.

They said nothing. They just looked at him with their hands in their pockets. The old Marlin looked up at the sky for a moment, then looked back down at his sneakers, wiggling one foot back and forth a little bit. A gull screeched.

"Oh, go ahead," the old Marlin finally thought.

Off flew overcoats, pants, shirts, and shoes in

all directions, and in jumped all the Marlins who had been standing on the pier. Morgan laughed and Spaceman laughed. Even the old Marlin smiled.

The water bubbled and churned where they had all leaped in, and Morgan could see nothing but their hats, which floated and bumped into one another on the surface of the water.

"Can they stay under long?" Morgan asked Spaceman.

"Not as long as you," he answered.

Morgan heard the other Marlins, who were watching the gate, yelling their thoughts across the parking lot. He backstroked across the surface and waved them on.

"What about us!"

"Hey, come on! That's not fair!"

"There's nobody coming! Why do we have to stay here!?"

The old Marlin yelled his thoughts back at them. "Five minutes! Five minutes and then get back to the gate!"

The Marlins at the gate ran across the parking lot, shedding their clothes as they raced to the water. When they hit the edge of the pier, they jumped as high as they could jump, which wasn't very high, and flopped backward into the water. Now all of them were underwater.

"Watch," Spaceman thought to Morgan. He dove under the water and Morgan followed him. The mud had settled some, but the water was still hazy. A brownish-yellow tint colored everything.

Morgan didn't see anything at first. Then he felt something swim quickly by behind him. He swung around to see who it was, but it was gone. Then another flash of white whisked by right in front of him. Everywhere Morgan looked, there were streaks of white flashes shooting by and floating bubbly trails left in their wake.

"Look how fast!" Morgan laughed.

The streaks of white turned flips, made figure eights, swam in formation, split off from one another, hugged the bottom, and skimmed the surface. They were going so fast that Morgan couldn't tell who was who. The Marlins flew by on all sides, yelling out thoughts and showing off to one another.

"Watch this!"

"My mother swims faster than you!"

"HA! You had to go up for air already!"

"Outta my way! I'm coming through!"

Every time Morgan turned to see who it was, he was already gone.

"Can I go with them!?" Morgan asked.

"Not yet."

The white streaks started to slow down. Gradually Morgan could make out the pink, little-boy bodies of the older Marlins swimming joyfully by in their white underwear. They came closer to Morgan and Spaceman and hovered over them, occasionally floating up to the surface for a quick breath. Their white undershorts billowed with the movement of the water. They smiled at Morgan.

For the first time, Morgan could clearly see the changes that had happened to each of them. Their bodies were all different. Some were pudgy and round, others wrinkled and skinny, but each had something of a Marlin about him. Patches of scales ran up and down most of their legs and along a few backs. Morgan saw sections of the leathery skin on some of them. A few toes were webbed together, and two of them had hands that had made the full change, but most of them had only one or two fingers webbed together. Little bits and pieces of Marlin spotted and freckled each of them.

"Can I go with you now? I'll race all of you!" Morgan thought to them as he finned out with a swoosh.

All the Marlins stopped swimming and stared at Morgan's fin. Their faces lost their smiles.

"What?" Morgan thought to them. "All right, I won't use my fin. I promise!"

Slowly, the Marlins all floated up to the surface and started to make their way out of the water.

"Hey, where're you going?" Morgan thought after them.

On the pier above, the old Marlin reached down and helped the men out of the water.

"What, are you mad because I have a fin and you don't? I don't believe you guys!"

"Morgan," the old Marlin thought, gently shaking his head.

It was that same voice, the one that had hummed through Morgan's body the first time he had seen the old Marlin on the side-walk back in the city. He remembered what the old Marlin had said to him that day. He turned to Spaceman.

"They stopped believing, didn't they?"

Spaceman said nothing.

"You did too, didn't you?"

Spaceman nodded his head yes.

"Why?"

Spaceman thought about this for a moment, and then he gently shook his head, shrugged his shoulders, and swam away.

Morgan didn't follow him. He sensed a quiet sadness in the Marlins, in all of them, sort of like the way he felt when he saw other kids in his neighborhood laughing and playing with their dads, a Sunday sort of sadness.

Morgan thought for a long time about this.

He didn't know why some people believed and some didn't, why some of the Marlins had only scales and others had hands and feet that were fully webbed, but he did know that if he were to stop believing in the middle of all this, it would be worse than never having believed at all.

CHAPTER TWENTY-FIVE

"**W**HAT ARE YOU DOING THERE?" Morgan asked Spaceman, who was busy rigging something up at the end of the pier.

"These are nets," Spaceman thought. "I'm stringing them along the pier so you don't go wandering off. We don't want you getting lost in the bay."

"I won't go far," Morgan thought as he turned to swim away.

"No you don't," thought Spaceman, grabbing Morgan's tail and pulling him back.

"He's right, Morgan," thought the old Marlin, walking up to the edge of the pier. "See all those marshes out there? Well, there's thousands of little channels that snake in and out of them. It would be the easiest thing in the world to take a wrong turn and never find your way back."

Spaceman let go of Morgan's tail and went

back to work on the rigging. Morgan swam a little closer to the pier. The old Marlin came over and sat down.

"Want to go for a swim?" asked Morgan. Spaceman chuckled under his breath.

"No, I don't. Listen to me now," the old Marlin thought.

"Okay."

"This is important."

"Okay."

"The bay is a safe place for fish. There's lots of places to hide if you have to."

"Hide?" asked Morgan, suddenly perking up.

"Yes, hide."

"From what?"

"I'll get to that. Just stick close to the pier for now."

"Are there other fish in the bay?"

"Many. This is where most fish come to have their children. They swim in through the Great Inlet to find a safe place for—"

"What's the Great Inlet?" asked Morgan impatiently.

"It's where the ocean meets the bay. You'll see it soon. The fish swim into the bay through the Great Inlet and raise their children in the quiet coves of the marshes, or in the hidden beds of eelgrass up in the shallows. Away from the dangers of the ocean."

"Dangers?" Morgan thought.

"Yes," the old Marlin thought seriously. "There's no place to hide in the ocean. The fish move in here so their children can grow up in safety, but when they are older, they have to swim out through the Great Inlet by themselves to live in the ocean. It's a big day for a fish when he leaves the bay for the open sea."

"And when do I do that?"

"Soon enough. You might want to learn how to swim first."

"Oh, I can swim just fine."

"Well, we'll see. Just remember, Morgan, everything is calmer and safer on the bay side of the inlet. Now, try to get used to your tail."

Morgan pushed off the pier with a flip of his fins and slammed into Spaceman.

"Sorry," Morgan thought, and tried swimming a little slower.

"You're not used to it yet," the old Marlin thought to him. "Take your time."

It was much harder than Morgan thought. When he had had two free legs with a flipper on the end of each, it had been easy to navigate. But now, with just one large tail, Morgan needed to learn all over again. It felt like trying to swim with your legs wrapped in a sleeping bag. Morgan swam off in awkward squary-looking circles, his arms flailing about at his sides as he tried to keep his balance.

"How do you keep from—" Morgan was asking when he suddenly turned sideways, fell to his right, and twisted in a lengthwise pirouette. He righted himself. "How do you stop twisting?" he asked Spaceman.

"Every Marlin swims differently," he answered. "Keep trying things—you'll learn."

Morgan kicked with his tail and bumped into Spaceman again. He tried to swim in slow circles, and that seemed to be a little easier, but every once in a while he would stall and sink to the bottom. When that happened, the old Marlin would think, loudly, "Do something!"

And Morgan would. It didn't always work. One time he slammed into the pier after too hard a kick with his tail, and another time he whapped his fin against one of the pilings. After a while, though, he could pretty much keep himself moving in a tight circle.

"Good!" thought Spaceman. "Take a break."

Morgan popped his head out of the water and looked around. Above the water, he could see, the net was strung about on all three sides. The fourth side was the pier, but underwater the net disappeared.

"I can't see the net when I'm underwater," Morgan thought.

Spaceman nodded his head. "Nets are one of the dangers of the open sea. You can't see them, but you can feel them. Try brushing against it. Feel it?"

"Yup."

"Good. Seeing isn't a very accurate sense anyway. We hardly ever use it."

The old Marlin bellowed out a thought from somewhere above. "Trust what you feel. Not what you see!"

"What?!" Morgan bellowed back.

No answer from the old Marlin.

"What's he talking about?" Morgan asked Spaceman, as he began circling again.

"Oh, that's just an old Marlin saying. Look, why don't you try to swim in straight lines. I think you've got circles handled."

Morgan stopped circling and backed up to the pier.

"Okay," thought Spaceman. "I want you to try to swim straight toward the net. When you feel it with the tip of your nose, dive slowly toward the bottom and throw your head back over your left shoulder. At the same time give a little kick with your tail. That should turn you around. Then swim toward the pier and do the same thing. Go on now."

Morgan spent most of that day getting used to not having legs. Or rather, getting used to *having* a tail. It wasn't as easy as he thought. He felt the net just fine, but when he dove toward the bottom, he wound up nose first in the mud. He had no idea how powerful his tail was, and how little effort he needed to move. The next time he kicked less, but he didn't dive deep enough and wound up tangled in the curtain of nets. Spaceman helped him out of it.

"Whoa, whoa! Don't kick! Don't flap around like that," he thought sternly.

"I can't get out of it," Morgan thought to him.

"Well . . . lesson number one," Spaceman thought quite seriously to Morgan. "This is what a net feels like. First thing you do if you get caught is stop. Don't move. Don't try to fight free of it. Just stop and gently try to back out the way you came in."

He set Morgan loose again and straightened out the net. Morgan popped out of the water to see who was watching. The old Marlin, still leaning against the car, thought to him, "It's not impossible to get out of a net. Most fish panic." He walked toward the front of the pier without unfolding his arms. "A Marlin doesn't panic."

Morgan swam back under.

"Why don't we work with the nets tomorrow," the old Marlin thought loudly. "Teach him to swim straight first!"

"I am swimming straight," Morgan thought back.

"Not very well."

"Don't get him mad," thought-whispered Spaceman to Morgan.

Morgan swam off a little and hit a piling. He floated slowly to the surface.

"That one hurt," he thought quietly.

"Well, don't kick so hard!" the old Marlin thought.

"When do we go to the ocean?" Morgan

thought to the old Marlin.

"You worry about not swimming into things," he thought back as he walked back to the car, "and I'll let you know when it's time for the ocean."

Morgan went back to practicing how to swim.

Spaceman stayed in the water with Morgan for most of the day. He gave Morgan lots of advice and encouragement, but more than anything, Morgan wanted the old Marlin to notice how well he was doing. He wanted him to jump off the hood of the car and think to everyone, "What a great Marlin! Did everyone see that?"

But he just sat on that car all day and stared.

So Morgan decided to leap.

He backed up to the front of the pier and took a few trial runs at the net. It was suspended from about two feet above the water. It didn't look very high to Morgan. He was sure he could clear it. He swam back to the pier again, turned around, and headed for the net. He stayed low to the bottom so he could get a good run up at the line. With two short kicks of his tail he was already right under it. He turned his nose up and headed to the surface.

One more great kick of his tail and he broke the water.

On his way out of the water, Morgan could see all the Marlins stop whatever they were doing and watch. Even the old Marlin looked surprised.

Morgan had no idea how powerful his body was becoming, and no idea how high a Marlin could leap. He cleared the net with ease.

And kept going up.

The leap was so high, and so fast, that Morgan had no control over it. He didn't know if he was upside down or sideways. He didn't even know where the water was. Everything was a tumbling blur of blue.

The first somersault took him high above the line. The second one started to twist and turn him back toward the pier, and by the time he fell back to the water, he had successfully performed a double-twisting back flip right onto his face. When he hit the water, he was so stunned that he started swimming as fast as he could. First he swam himself into a nosedive in the mud again. He pulled himself out and frantically started swimming crazy figure eights around the bay.

Morgan could see the other Marlins swimming out toward him, but he couldn't stop. Something in him just kept swimming as fast as he could. Eventually, one of the Marlins put himself in the path of one of Morgan's crazy eights, and Morgan plowed into him.

Spaceman came out and swam Morgan and the other Marlins toward the pier. He put Morgan back behind the nets.

Morgan stayed underwater for a while.

When he finally got enough nerve to come up again, he saw that the old Marlin was still sitting in the same spot on the car, looking the same way, with his arms still folded in the same position.

Morgan let himself slink back under the water.

He stayed there for a long time.

CHAPTER TWENTY-SIX

ALL THAT EVENING Morgan practiced swimming.

Back and forth behind the nets he experimented with his newfound fins and tail: learning how to glide, how to turn, how to stop.

Kicking with his tail always sent him shooting off so fast that he would lose control, so he tried different ways of moving it. He finally settled on wiggling his rear end from side to side. A quick wiggle, he called the first, and then just a wigg. One wigg was all he needed to move from one end of the pier to the other. If he wanted a little more speed, he would add a shimmy to the wigg. Actually, he added the shimmy between a wigg left and a wigg right. Morgan quickly learned that he had to offset a left wigg with a right wigg in order to keep going straight ahead. A single wigg by itself would always turn him in the direction of wherever he wigged from. So he would wigg left, and then wigg right. Then he added a shimmy in between the two for a little more speed. The shimmy was a side-to-side movement of just the tip of his tail.

Wigg left—shimmy—wigg right.

Over and over again he practiced. Then he added a shag to his shimmy, and now he was really moving.

A shag was a quick, muscular belly roll, like Hawaiian dancers do. A sudden shag undulated his whole body and shot him straight forward.

Wigg—shimmy—wigg—SHAG! Wigg— shimmy—wigg—SHAG!

Morgan couldn't help smiling where his mouth used to be. He still had a mouth, but not like the one he used to have. Morgan could feel that the corners of his lips had elongated and been pulled down and back, stretching the skin of his face tight. His lips had turned into a hard, leathery jawline that ran all the way down to where he used to have shoulders. They, too, were changing. They felt to him like they had come together in the middle. It was as if he'd tried to touch one shoulder to the other across the middle of his chest. Morgan's had met there, fused together, and streamlined his torso and legs into a torpedolike swimming machine. With each slight change to Morgan's body, he was able to move faster. And each time he moved faster, another little something would change. Little by little he was being shaped and molded into the perfect swimming machine.

SHAG! SHAG! SHAG!!

Faster and faster he shagged in figure eights and circles until the sun went down. Morgan continued to swim in the darkness, never once running into the nets anymore.

"Morgan," he heard from somewhere above. "Morgan!"

Morgan looked up through the watery haze. Stars in the sky high above flitted in and out of sight through the floating clouds of black silt he had stirred up below the surface. He heard the old Marlin at the pier's edge.

"Morgan, enough now. Try to get some rest. We have a big day tomorrow."

"Watch this!" Morgan thought without thinking, and shimmy-shagged around the berth.

"Morgan!" the old Marlin thought again. "That's very good. You learn fast. Now rest.

Even Marlins need rest."

"Okay."

"Oh, Morgan."

"Yes?"

"When's the last time you had to come up for air?"

"I don't anymore."

"Rest now," the old Marlin said, and headed back to the car.

Morgan tried to swim sleep, but his mind was racing. He thought about exploring the bay and meeting other fish, of leaping off waves, of swimming through the Great Inlet, and of living in the open sea.

The water was black—blacker than any black Morgan had ever seen. He thought about what lay beyond his nets in the floating darkness. He thought about leaving his parents and being on his own. And then he thought about the other Marlins swimming around in their underwear and laughing.

He smiled at the thought.

CHAPTER TWENTY-/EVEN

MORNING CAME SLOWLY to the dark waters. Morgan studied a shaft of sunlight as it crept down one of the pilings in his berth. It fell to the bottom of the bay and lit up a little triangle of mud, crabs, and shells that lay littered on the bottom. He shag swam over to it, nestled into it like a cat in a window, and sat on a flounder.

"Excuse me," Morgan thought to it. But it didn't think back. It flippity-flopped in a little floating somersault and willowed away.

Looking up through the water, Morgan watched the rippling sky above begin to blue.

"This is what the sky looks like to a Marlin," he thought, delighted.

The sun ever so slowly rolled out a carpet of light across the muddy bottom of the bay as if not to disturb anything that might still be sleeping. Morgan could see and hear hundreds of other living things that were under the water with him. Little calico crabs click-clicked their claws at each other. Zigzagging sheets of silver whisked in and around him as tiny schools of baby fish darted by. A young blowfish sauntered in, puffing himself up to look very important. Jellyfish drifted, clams spit, scallops scalloped, and minnows minnowed. Then something floated in front of Morgan's eyes.

He tried to swim under it, but it followed him. He tried to swim around it, but it did the same thing. It looked like a stick or an old fishing pole floating in front of him. He tried to bat it away and hit himself in the face.

"Ow!—that's me!" he thought. "I mean—it's—that's mine! It's attached to me!"

He felt where his nose used to be.

It was now a bill. It had grown out of what used to be his upper lip and stretched out to a tapered point in front of him to become the bill that makes Marlins distinctly Marlins.

"Yes!" he thought to himself.

He nosed it into the pier and scraped a mark into the wood. He tapped it across an old clam shell, and the shell broke. Quickly, he felt around his head to see what else had changed.

His bald head was still bald and felt the same. His ears were gone. His—

"Ears! Ears are gone!"

He felt where his ears should be, and they weren't. Then he slid his hands farther along his neck. There were two narrow slits running across both sides.

They were gills.

He ran his finny hands along the edges of his gills. They were sharp and hard, like armor plating. He thrashed his head back and forth. The little fish around him swam for cover and the crabs buried themselves in the mud.

Morgan felt powerful.

"HEY!" thought down the old Marlin. "Hey, what's all the splashing about?"

Morgan pointed his bill up toward the surface and periscoped it out of the water. Then he popped up, and if he had had a mouth that could smile, he would have. He was smiling inside, though.

"I got my bill overnight!" he thought. "And my gills. Look!"

He twisted his bobbing head left and right to show the old Marlin his gills. Then he twisted completely around in a swishing circle and dove under the water. He popped up closer to the pier, right under the old Marlin. The sun was sneaking up behind the silhouetted old Marlin and the others, who were gathering at the edge of the pier.

"Hey everyone," Morgan thought out. "Rise and shine!"

The ragged Marlins shuffled closer to the pier, sleepy eyed and rumpled.

"He's got his bill and gills," the old Marlin announced to the group.

Morgan could see them all suddenly become very awake. They shook the sleep out of their heads and rushed to the edge of the pier to see. Morgan shagged back and forth to show everyone.

"Already?!"

"He just *tailed* yesterday!"

"He's changing faster than I thought," the old Marlin thought over his shoulder.

The other Marlins nodded heads in agreement as they crowded around to get a better look. The sun was peeking over their shoulders.

"Okay, let's get this show on the road," the old Marlin thought to everyone. "The full moon is in two days. He's got to be ready for the Inlet by then. You two go for the boat. You three on nets. Somebody else on lures."

Instantly the Marlins divided up into their assigned groups and went to work. The Marlins going for the boat hopped into the car. They put their sunglasses on, pulled their hats down on their foreheads, and cinched up their overcoats.

"We'll be back in a few hours," they thought, and drove away.

"What's going on?" Morgan thought loudly.

"We've got a lot to do today," Spaceman thought as he jumped into the water with Morgan. "You're changing faster than we expected. You can't stay here much longer."

"Why not?"

"Well, if we stay here too long, someone is bound to see us, but more important, there's a full moon on its way."

"So?"

"We told you about the Great Inlet, right?"

"Yes."

"Well, we're going to get you through the Inlet on an outgoing tide with a full moon. That's when the tide is the strongest. It's the best chance you'll have. You'll be open-sea free in no time."

"Open-sea free!"

"Yup."

"Hurry it up down there!" the old Marlin thought loudly from above.

"All right!" Spaceman thought back. Then he turned to Morgan. "I'll tell you more later. Right now, let's get you out of here."

"Where are we going?!"

"Out into the bay."

Spaceman finished taking down the nets. Then he took off most of his clothes and swam out past Morgan. That was when Morgan saw Spaceman's back for the first time. From the neck down, he was completely covered with scales. They glittered down his shoulders and across the backs of his arms, down his back, and across the backs of both legs right down to his heels. They flashed and sparkled as he twisted his body in circles around Morgan. Both his feet were webbed, and he even had the smallest beginnings of a fin down the center of his back. It was just a little one—just a little ridge that ran down his spine—but it was definitely a fin.

Morgan couldn't help but stare. He looked up, and Spaceman smiled a tiny smile at him.

"I almost made it," he thought to Morgan.

They both hovered there a moment looking at each other under the water, and then in a flash Spaceman was gone. Nothing was left but a cloud of fizzy bubbles that floated slowly to the surface. Then just as quickly as he was gone, he was back in front of Morgan's face.

"What are you waiting for?" he thought to Morgan, and swam off again.

Morgan followed this time, and fell in alongside him.

"Follow me," Spaceman thought over to him. "We'll take a few laps around the cove."

Morgan swam shoulder to shoulder with Spaceman. When he turned, Morgan turned; when he kicked his legs, Morgan kicked his tail. They swam as one.

"How do we do that?" Morgan asked of the swimming in unison.

"No one knows," answered Spaceman as Morgan and he both headed up to skim along the surface.

"See, like that! How did we both know to come up at the same time?!"

"You got me!"

They both slow skimmed the surface of the cove.

"Coves almost always have water that's very calm," Spaceman thought as they swam along. "They're a good place to ditch into when there's a storm. And . . . there's plenty of food to be found here."

"Food!?" Morgan thought. "I forgot about food. I'm starved."

"Well, do you like squid?"

"Squid?! You're joking, right?"

"Nope."

Spaceman darted off, and Morgan followed behind. The bottom of the cove started to angle down, and they both followed it, swimming deeper. It leveled off again, and they swam slowly along.

"Look up," Spaceman said.

"What?"

"Look up."

Morgan twisted his body to the left and looked up. A great cloud of silvery white floated above them. Spaceman made a quick move with his hand, and the silvery cloud shot off like a flock of spooked sparrows.

"That'd be squid," Spaceman said with a smile. "C'mon."

Morgan and Spaceman swam up behind the

school and followed them. The squid tried to turn and dart away; they backtracked and U-turned, dove deep, and shot above, but Morgan and Spaceman mirrored their every move.

"Well, go ahead," Spaceman thought to Morgan. "There's breakfast."

"I'm not eating that!"

"Oh, just try it, you big baby," thought Spaceman as he pushed Morgan ahead of him.

"Couldn't I start with . . . like . . . clams or something?"

"This is what Marlins eat. Now, go on."

"Squid for breakfast . . ."

Morgan swam up a little closer to the school.

"Snap, crackle, *squid* . . ." he thought over his shoulder. "Mmm!"

"Just go on," thought Spaceman at him.

Morgan gave a big kick with his tail and swam up closer to the school. Again they dodged and ducked through the water, trying to lose Morgan, but he stayed with every turn. He followed the squid for a while, wondering to himself how he knew exactly which way they were going to move and when. Spaceman stayed close behind him.

"At night," thought Spaceman to him, "squid are phosphorescent."

"They glow in the dark!?"

"Yup."

"Get outta here!"

"They do. When you run through a big school of them out in the ocean, they scatter and flash purple blues and yellow greens like big underwater fireflies. The whole ocean lights up."

"Cool."

Morgan swam closer to the school as they tried, yet again, to throw him off their track.

"Go on already!" Spaceman thought.

Into the middle of the school flew Morgan. Squid were everywhere. They swam into Morgan, they swam over him, they darted and whizzed in all directions. Morgan chomped blindly left and right trying to catch one, missing every time. He followed one down toward the bottom and lunged after it, missed, and plunged himself into a bed of seaweed. He came up dazed and shook the seaweed off his bill.

Spaceman was laughing all the way up to get air. He swam back down to Morgan.

"Well, now I'll teach you how to do it the

right way," he thought with a smile. "Come on."

They caught up to the school again and fell in behind them.

"All you have to do," Spaceman thought over to Morgan, "is use your bill."

"What are you talking about?"

"Next time you swim through the school, thrash your bill around. It'll slow a few of them down. Then circle back and nab a snack."

Off Morgan went again.

He swam through the school of squid and flailed his bill from side to side. Then he circled back and opened his mouth wide.

"Hey," Morgan thought to Spaceman. "My mouth! I can open my mouth again!"

It was the first time he had completely opened his mouth since the day he had left his apartment for the hospital.

"It works!" Morgan continued joyfully. He stretched his strong jaws open as far as possible. "Ha! Look at this! Look how wide I can—!"

A huge gulp of water sucked itself down Morgan's throat, along with four squid.

"Ggargharg!" gagged Morgan.

"Good!" thought Spaceman.

"Sq—squid . . ." Morgan gargled out. "I . . .

I ate a squid—oh, gross . . . I ate squid for breakfast!" Morgan added a few more choking sounds for effect. "Hey . . . hey, you know, they taste pretty good."

Spaceman chuckled.

"I'm going to try that again," Morgan thought as he swam off. He was back in a flash, having gulped down another two squid.

"Not bad, huh?" asked Spaceman.

"Nope," thought Morgan with a swallow. "It's kind of squishy, but not bad."

"You learn fast," complimented Spaceman. "That's good. We've got a lot to do in the next few hours. Hey, wait—"

Morgan swam after the school again.

"That's enough," Spaceman thought after him. "Come on, we've got lots to do."

Morgan chased the school of squid again and again. They split off in different directions and tried to escape each time Morgan plunged into them. Each time he did, they divided themselves into smaller and smaller groups, until the school was scattered into tiny clusters.

"Morgan!" thought Spaceman. "Take only what you need to eat!"

"There's one by itself. Watch this!" Morgan

thought over his shoulder as he swam after another squid.

"Morgan, don't! That's not a—"

"A little squid over easy," Morgan thought to himself as he fell in behind the lonesome squid. "Should have stuck with the crowd, little guy."

Morgan sucked the squid into his mouth. No sooner had he done so than something sharp and pointed stabbed into the top of his jaw.

"OW!"

It plunged in deeper. It cut into Morgan's jaw and started pulling him toward the shore.

"Ow! Help! Help!" Morgan screamed. He thrashed his head and pulled back, but when he did, the something sharp dug in deeper. It burned the inside of his mouth and sent shooting pains down the length of his neck.

Spaceman flew through the water and swam in front of Morgan. He broke through the surface of the water.

"Stop reeling!" he thought-yelled out. "Stop reeling—you've got Morgan! You've hooked Morgan!"

Morgan crashed through the surface of the water and flung his head from side to side. One of the Marlins onshore was pulling back on a fishing pole. He didn't hear Spaceman or see Morgan. Spaceman quickly turned back to Morgan. "Swim with it, Morgan. Swim with it and it'll take the pressure off."

"I can't—it hurts."

"Do it NOW!"

Morgan swam hard in the direction he was being pulled. The pain lessened as he did. He swam into it a little more, and the fishing line brushed along the length of his bill, sliding up toward his eye.

"Wrap it around your bill," thought Spaceman to him. "Swim into the line a little more and wrap it around your bill!"

Morgan did as he was told. He swam hard in the direction he was being pulled. He felt the thin monofilament line slide over his bill. He flung his head in a wide circle and wrapped the line around his bill.

"Turn sideways now!" Spaceman yelled at him. "Turn your head to the side and swim off!"

Morgan turned tail and began to swim away. The fishing line tightened around his bill and dug into his skin.

"Use your head, Morgan!" Spaceman yelled

after him. "Your head!"

The line straightened taut and quivered in the water. Morgan dropped his head back in the direction of the shore. The line went slack for just a moment, and then Morgan flung his head hard and high out of the water in the opposite direction. The line tightened and sang in the air for a split second, then snapped with a sharp crack. Morgan saw the Marlin on land fall backward into the marshes just as he, himself, fell back into the water. Spaceman swam over and helped untangle the swirl of fishing line that was strung around Morgan's bill.

"What was that?" Morgan asked, quite shaken.

"That was a *lure*."

Spaceman helped Morgan swim into shore. Once back by the pier, Morgan rested on the bottom. Spaceman broke through the surface and started screaming his thoughts at the Marlin with the fishing pole.

The Marlin yelled back apologetically. "I was just trying to get the knots out of the line!"

"Morgan," the old Marlin thought.

Morgan slow-floated to the surface. The old Marlin motioned for Morgan to come over to him. Morgan did. "Throw me down the pliers," he thought to another Marlin, and lowered himself into the water with Morgan.

Morgan sat quietly. No one thought anything for a moment.

"I could use a hand here," the old Marlin thought. "Hold his head for me."

Spaceman took hold of Morgan by the gills.

"This is going to hurt a bit," the old Marlin thought, and grabbed the hook with his pliers.

"Aurgh . . . aghrga," replied Morgan.

The old Marlin popped out the hook.

"OW!"

"Well," thought the old Marlin to Morgan, holding up a mangled squid lure, "did you learn anything by this?"

"Yeah, stick to cereal for breakfast."

"Very funny. This was going to be one of your lessons, although we weren't actually going to hook you. Now," thought the old Marlin, dangling the lure in front of Morgan's bill. "What's the first thing about this lure that's different from a real squid?"

"It's plastic, for one thing!"

"True, but that's hard to see from underwater. What else?"

239

"Well, it's got three huge *hooks* hanging from it. I guess that's a pretty good clue."

"That too, but you can't see it underwater when it's moving. What did you notice first about it when you saw it in the water?"

Morgan thought for a moment.

"It was alone."

"Right. Never eat anything that swims alone," the old Marlin thought to him. "Did it swim left and right to get away from you?"

"No, just straight ahead."

"Clue number two. Never eat anything that doesn't do well at getting away from you."

"I thought it was just a dumb squid."

"No, that's what we call a dumb Marlin."

"And never take more than you need to," added Spaceman.

"Morgan," thought the old Marlin, "you did well breaking away once you were caught, though. I have to say that. That's a trick it can take some Marlins years to learn."

The old Marlin climbed out of the water. Spaceman followed him. Morgan settled on the bottom for a moment and thought about what the old Marlin had just said.

His jaw didn't hurt that much anymore.

CHAPTER TWENTY-EIGHT

OR THE REST OF THE MORNING and into the afternoon, Spaceman taught Morgan about all kinds of lures and nets. Morgan learned about lures that scooted and popped across the surface, and heard about others that dove under the water and wiggled, and even some that swam and sank to the bottom to look like a wounded fish.

"They're all meant to trick you," Spaceman warned Morgan. "Now, let's go over the nets again."

"Again?" Morgan complained.

"A Marlin never stops learning."

"All right," Morgan thought, shrugging his dorsal fin.

"We're not playing around here, Morgan. We're teaching you how to survive on your own."

"On my own," Morgan thought quietly to

himself. He had never been on his own before. He had never really been without his parents.

"Come on, I'll quiz you," continued Spaceman. *"Gill nets."*

"They float in one spot," Morgan recited, "usually submerged. . . . Um . . . back out right away. Don't panic."

"Good," thought Spaceman. *"Purse nets."*

"They try to circle the net around you and pull it closed like tying you up in a bag. It hangs from a bunch of buoys. All you gotta do is swim in the center of the net until the mouth of it is almost closed, then look for the buoys that float the net and leap over them."

"Make sure you're deep enough to get a good leap," Spaceman added.

"Oh, yeah, hug the bottom of the net."

"There's a lot to remember, I know," Spaceman thought.

"Are these nets and lures and things everywhere?"

"No, but you have to assume that they are. There aren't supposed to be any in the bay, but people sneak in and do it anyway. They usually try to catch the fish carrying eggs—because they're slower."

"That's awful."

"So even in the bay you have to be watch-ful. But out in the deep sea you shouldn't have too much to worry about. Most of the ocean nets are within a few hundred miles of shore. You just need to stay out at sea, don't feed close to shore, and avoid boats—" Spaceman stopped talking and tapped Morgan on his bill. "Are you listening?"

Morgan didn't answer.

"What is it, Morgan?"

Morgan smelled something funny.

It was something he'd smelled many times before, but he couldn't quite place it. Then he heard a low, distant rumble. The rumble got louder and louder. Morgan backed up to the pier and slunk down to the floor of the bay again. Then an unmistakable whiff of diesel fuel shot through his body. He had smelled it almost every day of his life, standing on the street corner as newspaper trucks, bread trucks, and city buses spewed by him.

There was a boat coming into the cove.

At first Morgan panicked, but then he remembered that some of the other Marlins had left earlier to go get a boat. Morgan popped his head out of the water to watch it putt-putt through the narrow opening of the cove. The boat bobbed up and down and splashed little splashes of white spray each time it did. Some of the Marlins were leaning over the bow railing, trying to catch the spray in their hands. The cowboy-hatted Marlin was steering. The others were in the back of the boat, sitting on the rail.

"Let's get that net over here!" Morgan heard the old Marlin think somewhere up above. Morgan turned to see the Marlins dragging over a net they had stretched out and untangled in the parking lot.

"Down to the end of the pier," the old Marlin continued. "And then get on the boat."

The Marlins up above pulled the great net down to the end of the pier. Spaceman swam out to meet the boat, which was idling in a little closer now.

Morgan started to follow, but a sharp, sudden pain behind his eyes stopped him.

"Ah!" he cried out, but Spaceman didn't hear him.

Morgan pressed his finny hands against his head and slunk to the bottom of the bay. His forehead thrummed with pain. It pulled at his eyes and seared down the back of his neck. It felt as if his head were about to explode, and then it stopped.

Something was different.

Morgan wasn't quite sure what it was at first. He couldn't see very well. Everything was a little fuzzy. He shook his bill from side to side, trying to clear his head. The water looked muddy, but it wasn't. He shook his bill again and stared hard through the water. Slowly, things began to come into focus again. As they did, Morgan could see things he had never seen before. Not only could Morgan see in front, but he could see to both sides and behind himself too.

Morgan's head had changed.

His eyes had pulled themselves back and had come to rest on either side of his head, sort of where his ears used to be. Morgan had almost a three-hundred-sixty-degree view. If he turned both eyes to the front, it was like focusing binoculars. There were two separate views that tried to melt into one. They stopped, however, about two inches before they merged. There Morgan saw either side of a little hump, which was the beginning of his bill. It made him dizzy to look at it. The bill split his view down the middle, but if he followed it out to the end and then looked beyond, things came into focus again.

He could do the same thing if he looked behind him. He turned his eyes toward the back, and his tail split the picture in the middle. He could see anything from any direction. He swam out and shagged over to the boat. It was now tied up to the end of the pier, and all the Marlins were on board. Morgan popped up alongside it.

"Hey, there!" thought cowboy hat. "Look at you!"

"His head!" thought the wool-capped Marlin. "Look where his eyes are!"

Morgan spun like a top in the water, showing off his latest change.

"I can see everywhere!" he thought to them.

All the Marlins looked over at Morgan. The boat creaked and leaned to the same side as they did, as if it were straining to look too.

"Good," thought the old Marlin. "I was hoping you'd have your eyes fully before we ran you through the nets."

"Through the nets?" Morgan asked.

"Yup," answered the old Marlin, "we're going to—"

A car drove up to the gate.

"Get down!" the old Marlin quickly thought to everyone.

Everyone ducked down in the back of the boat. Morgan and Spaceman dove under the water. They swam closer to the pier, floated up to the surface, and peeked out over the parking lot.

"Do you know that car?" asked Spaceman.

"No," thought Morgan.

The car idled at the gate. It waited for a moment. Then it hesitantly backed up and drove off. Everyone popped up from the back of the boat.

"Who was that?"

"I don't know."

"Could just be a fisherman."

"Okay," thought the old Marlin. "Let's get back to—"

The car screeched back into view, in reverse, and banged into the loose gates, flinging them open. It was too quick for anyone to hide. The car continued between the swinging gates, squealing and scrunching over the shell-strewn parking lot. It swerved and snaked toward the edge of the pier, then it screeched to a halt about five feet from the water. No one moved in the car. Suddenly the driver's-side door was flung open.

"Well, reverse and second gear are right next to each other," Molly said apologetically.

"You drive-a like a crazy lady!" Mrs. Pasalaqua said, unruffling herself as she nearly fell out of the passenger side. "I drive-a next time!"

Morgan's father stepped out of the car. He opened the back door and helped Morgan's mother out.

"Mom! Dad!" Morgan thought loudly, but they didn't hear him. "Over here!"

"There they are!" Molly yelled.

Morgan's father spied the Marlins at the end of the pier. He walked over. Briskly. Mom followed close behind with Molly and Mrs. Pasalaqua. "Where's my son!?" his father asked angrily into the crowd. "Where is he!?"

"He's safe," the old Marlin thought calmly. "He's right here."

"Who said that?" asked his father. "Who—?"

"I did," the old Marlin quietly thought to Morgan's father, who stared suspiciously at him.

"I told you," Molly said. "It's how they talk."

Morgan swam out a little from the pier so they could see him better and waved at his mom and dad—*tried* to wave.

His arms had disappeared.

The last change had happened. His arms had joined into the rest of his sleek Marlin body. His hands were two fins that flared out from where his hips used to be.

Morgan was now all Marlin.

He splashed about in the water and leaped little leaps to get his parents' attention. His father peered out at the commotion. His mother stepped closer to the edge of the pier and stared out.

"Morgan?" she whispered, ever so softly.

Morgan spun like a top, flip-flapped his fins, and swam back to the pier.

"Yes," thought the old Marlin. "That's Morgan."

"You tell me what you've done with my son!" Morgan's father threatened. "If you—"

"Hi, Morgan!" Molly said as she walked to the edge of the pier. Her hair fell in front of her face as she leaned toward the water. She held it out of her eyes with both hands. "Well, look at you. If you aren't the little fish—*Marlin*, I mean, sorry. Why, just look at you."

"It'sa a miracle!" Mrs. Pasalaqua whispered. "I'm-a no crazy like-a Missy Molly—I tella you, I see a miracle."

"*Everyone's* crazy!" his father yelled. "I want to know where my son is!"

Morgan swam a little closer and bobbed up and down in the water right under where his mother was. He pushed his pointy bill up as far as he could and let it waver there. He twisted his body slightly to the side, and his mother looked into one of his eyes.

"Morgan?" she said, beginning to believe.

Morgan nodded his bill up and down in confirmation.

"Oh, my god," she said. She reached out and touched his bill.

"It's real! I'm real!" Morgan said, but she couldn't understand him. He was still silent to his parents' ears.

"This is ridiculous! I'm going to get the

police right now!" he father hollered as he stormed back to the car. "I'm going to have all of you—"

"DAD!" Morgan thought as hard as he could.

His father stopped in his tracks. He turned around slowly.

"Mor— Morgan?" he said quietly.

"He understood me," thought Morgan.

"Yes, he did," answered the old Marlin.

"Dad . . . it's me," Morgan continued. "I'm right here."

His father walked back to the edge of the pier and looked down at Morgan.

"Hi, Dad . . . it's really me," he thought to him gently. "I'm a Marlin."

Morgan's father stared in silence. All the other Marlins on the boat schooled up and remained very quiet. Spaceman climbed up on a corner of the pier and watched from a distance. Morgan's mother and Molly held each other and stared at him. Mrs. Pasalaqua beamed and kissed a medallion that hung around her neck. They, too, could understand Morgan now.

"Remember, I told you I wanted to be a Marlin?" Morgan continued. "And you said I could be anything I want?"

His mother and father both slowly nodded their heads yes.

"Well, it worked. I'm a Marlin."

"You're a—a—fish?" his father asked quietly.

"A *Marlin*," Molly said, gently correcting him.

"This is crazy! You're all nuts!" he hollered.

"It's true, Dad."

"Oh, it is, is it? You're Morgan? You're—you're going to swim there and tell me that—I can't believe this—look at me! Look at me! I'm talking to a fish! I'm talking to a—*oh my, god, I am talking to a fish.*"

His father stopped talking.

And started to understand.

He sat down on the pier. His mother sat next to him. Molly and Mrs. Pasalaqua sat next to her.

Everyone was beginning to understand one another.

CHAPTER TWENTY-NINE

MORGAN TOLD HIS PARENTS everything.

He told them about the first time he'd seen the Great Marlin in the vision he had had in the living room, of seeing the old man on the stoop, and of the first changes he'd noticed in the bathtub back in the city. They sat, rapt, with their legs hanging over the pier.

"I don't understand it either," Morgan thought, sensing their disbelief. "But it happened. I mean, look at me . . . I'm a Marlin."

No one could argue with that.

"Watch!" he cried out as he back-shagged out into the cove. His dorsal fin ripped through the water and disappeared, leaving a skinny wake of white that fanned out and faded across the water. He dove to the bottom, circled once to gather up speed, and headed for the surface. He broke the water with a great splash of shimmering blue and white, twisted his body, and reeled his great Marlin head from side to side. He fell back to the water with an even bigger splash and shimmy-shagged back over to the pier. He bobbed up under his mother's feet and poked her white shoe with the tip of his bill.

"Pretty good, huh?" he asked.

"Yes," his mother answered.

His father looked over toward the boat full of Marlin men and stood up. Morgan knew his father didn't see Marlins. He knew he couldn't see the swirling blue of the ocean in their once-wild eyes. He saw a bunch of guys in ratty overcoats who had turned his son into a fish.

"I want to know who you guys are!"

"Dad, don't yell," Morgan pleaded.

"Look, I don't know what's going on here, but I want some answers. Now!" yelled his father, walking toward the boat full of Marlins. They schooled up and backed against the far rail. The boat leaned in the same direction, following them.

"WELL!?" he yelled again.

"No one has done anything to Morgan," the old Marlin thought, walking between his father and the boat. "Morgan has changed because he wished to."

"Because he *wished* to?" his father echoed sarcastically. "Because he *wished to!!?*"

"Yes."

"Well, I wish I was six foot tall! You don't see me *sprouting*, do you! Do you!!?"

"Please stop yelling," Morgan thought to his father.

"It's not that kind of wishing," the old Marlin thought calmly.

"Well, what kind is it then? You tell me!"

"Morgan believed in something and became it. We don't know how to explain it, why some of us *become* and some of us don't."

"This isn't happening," Dad mumbled quietly under his breath.

"But it *has* happened," continued the old Marlin, staying very calm. "I know what you're feeling. *We* all doubted too. That's why none of us ever made it."

"Made what?" his father asked.

The old Marlin glanced back at the Marlins on the boat. They all nodded to one another and stepped forward.

The old Marlin and the others rolled up their sleeves, opened their shirts, and pulled up a pant leg or two. They held their hands outstretched, palms up, laying bare their marks of the Marlin. They showed them off proudly, like scars of battle from a once-sacred war. Patches of scales glittered out from under their wrinkled clothes, a few webbed hands waved, someone stuck out a finny foot and wiggled it.

Molly helped Morgan's mother and Mrs. Pasalaqua up off the pier. They walked over and stood behind Morgan's dad. The four of them stared in hushed wonder.

"I told you," Molly whispered in Dad's ear.

The old Marlin helped Morgan's dad to a picnic table that sat, rotted and initial carved, by the water's edge. He sat down with him. Molly, Mom, and Mrs. Pasalaqua joined them.

"I don't understand it either," the old Marlin thought comfortingly. "None of us do. I thought I was going crazy when it first happened to me. It scared me, and I stopped believing. And then I stopped *becoming*. Same as the rest of us."

The school nodded in unison.

"Morgan never stopped believing."

Everyone was silent for a long time.

Morgan wanted to say something, but nothing came out. His mother sat, hands on chin, gazing at him. His father sat, head bowed, twisting his wedding ring.

"We all came from the sea," the old Marlin continued. "And we'll all return to it, one way or another. It's there for any of us who can hear it call."

"I don't hear anything," Morgan's father said a little gruffly.

"Have you ever listened for it?" asked the old Marlin gently.

Everyone was silent again. After a moment Morgan's father looked up from the table.

"I think you're all insane. This is insane."

"Maybe so," thought the old Marlin. "But there's Morgan." He gestured to Morgan. Morgan waved his bill at his dad. "And that is a Marlin that's waving his bill at you. Now, you can explain it any way you want."

Morgan's dad got up from the picnic table and walked over to the edge of the pier. He looked at his blue-billed son.

"Morgan, is that really you?" he asked.

"Yes, Dad. It's really me."

His father shook his head slightly, as if trying

to convince himself that he was indeed insane, and looked back at the old Marlin. After an awkward silence, he said, "Well, I don't know— maybe. I mean, even if what you say is true . . . what do we do now? So my son is a fish and has the knowledge of the universe or something, so what? How's that going to help him make a living? What's he going to do with that when we get him home?"

"Home?" the old Marlin thought. "Morgan *is* home. That's the whole point of all of this. He needs to be released."

"Released?!" his mother asked fearfully. "What do you mean?"

"Released where?" added his dad.

"The ocean."

"The ocean!?" his mother exclaimed.

"But . . . but . . ." his father said. "He— It's too dangerous! He can't go."

"Yes, it's too dangerous," said his mom. "We'll take him back home."

"He can't go back," thought the old Marlin. "He's changed."

"Well . . ." his dad said, searching, "we'll get him a pool or something. Or . . ."

"He could live at the Y," his mom suggested.

"Yes," said Dad, "we'll get him a room at the Y. They've got a big pool."

"Please, listen to me," the old Marlin thought to them both. "Morgan can't live in a swimming pool. He can't even live in a bay as big as this. He needs the ocean."

"But the doctors said they could help him," Morgan's mom said. "We've never given them a real chance."

"Yes," his father agreed.

Molly jumped in. "They want to cut his fin off!" she said. "I heard them talking!"

"NO!" Morgan cried out. "NO!!" he thought again, and hid under the surface of the water.

"It's okay, honey," his mom said, trying to soothe him. "No one is going to take your . . . your fin." She stopped and said to herself, "Listen to me."

The old Marlin walked up to Morgan's mother. "If the doctors get their hands on him, they will take away everything that makes Morgan who he is. They will rob him of what he has become—a Marlin."

All the Marlins and Molly nodded in unison. No one spoke.

Morgan's mother and father looked at each other.

The water lapped against the side of the pier.

After a long moment Morgan's mother and father spoke to each other at the same time.

"Oh, no" was what they said.

"What?" asked the old Marlin.

"The doctors," his father said. "I told them where we were."

The Marlins in the boat rustled nervously.

"How long ago?" asked the old Marlin.

"Just before we left," answered his father. "I called them as we were leaving the house."

The Marlins on the boat nervously whispered thoughts to each other. Spaceman paced back and forth along the pier, peering toward the open gate. The old Marlin stepped close to Morgan's mother and father and spoke seriously to them.

"You have to let Morgan go." He waited for their answer. "Will you help us?"

Morgan looked at his parents.

They both nodded their heads yes. In unison.

CHAPTER THIRTY

ALL WAS CHAOS.

The Marlins bustled back and forth, gathering up their belongings and stowing away gear.

"Stay underwater," the old Marlin thought to Morgan. He turned to Morgan's father. "We'll have to move the plans up a bit."

"What can I do?" Morgan's father asked.

"Move that car, to begin with," thought the old Marlin. "Down to the end of the parking lot, so they can't see it from the road."

Morgan's father jumped into the car and did as the old Marlin asked. Morgan swam the length of the pier, staying alongside the car as his father drove it. He breached the surface every now and then with a little splash. His father watched him from the window. He parked the car and started walking back to the boat. Again Morgan swam along next to him.

"Let's hurry it up down there!" the old

Marlin shouted along the pier.

Morgan's father started to run. He was panting and breathing heavily. He crackled over broken shells and wiped his brow as he trotted along. Between gasps he looked at Morgan butterflying through the water alongside him.

"This is—*(pant)*—crazy!" he said to Morgan with a little laugh.

"I know!" Morgan thought back.

They both arrived back at the boat at the same time.

"Morgan!" Molly called. "I found this in your room at the hospital."

Morgan swam over to the dock.

"I don't have a lot of patients who leave fishing tackle behind," she said, holding out the great silvery hook. "I thought it was probably yours."

Morgan looked up at the hook and remembered that this wasn't a dream . . . and that he had no hands.

"Give it to my father," Morgan thought to her, and she did.

"What's this?" Dad asked.

"It's from Morgan," Molly answered.

Morgan's father smiled a soft smile and put the hook into his pocket.

"You're going to need these," the old Marlin thought as he tossed four life preservers to Molly.

"What about the tide?" asked cowboy hat.

"We can't wait. We've got to get him out now."

Molly, Mrs. Pasalaqua, and Morgan's parents trussed themselves up in the orange life preservers and boarded the boat.

"This boat is-a filthy," Mrs. Pasalaqua said, shaking her head at the old Marlin. "I clean."

Molly helped some of the older Marlins find places to sit, coiled up ropes, and checked pulses. "You should lie down up front," she said to one of the older Marlins as she felt his forehead. "You're a little warm."

"I think it's just the hat," he thought back politely.

"I know. Don't you just hate them?"

"Morgan," the old Marlin thought, "swim out into the cove a bit and wait for us there."

Morgan did as he was told. He shagged out a ways and turned to watch the boat rumble and sputter in the water as the old Marlin gunned the engines. A billowy puff of black smoke coughed out the exhausts.

That was when everyone heard the sirens.

Morgan popped his head farther out of the water. The old Marlin stopped what he was doing and looked up, and everyone on the boat listened.

Yes, it was definitely sirens.

"This is it!" shouted the old Marlin. "Throw those bowlines off!"

The Marlin with the cowboy hat went to throw off the lines, but Molly scampered around the side of the boat and beat him there. She untied the lines and tossed them aside.

"Bowlines off!" she volleyed back to the old Marlin.

The sirens were getting closer. Morgan looked up and saw two police cars and an ambulance screeching to a stop just inside the gate. Lights flashed, doors opened, and sirens screamed. Out of the cars piled people dressed in either all blue or all white. A lone white coat walked away from the group and peered across the parking lot. Then it looked out over the water.

"There they are!" Morgan heard Dr. Reichart yell. "That's them!"

They all jumped back into their cars and headed for the end of the pier.

The old Marlin pushed the throttle forward. Everyone held on tight as the boat
lurched forward.

"Morgan!" shouted the old Marlin. "Stay
behind the boat and follow us out."

Morgan shimmied back and fell in behind
the boat. "I can't see anything!" he thought to the
old Marlin, popping his head out of the water.

"You're too close to the wake," he shot
back. "Drop back a little."

Morgan stopped swimming for a moment
and let the boat pull ahead. The foamy white
wake fizzed out, and he could see again.

"THIS IS THE POLICE," megaphoned a
man in blue from the edge of the pier. Red
beams flashed behind the crowd of people
gathered on the dock. "TURN THE BOAT
AROUND AND RETURN TO THE PIER!"

No one said anything. Morgan swam quietly.
The boat sputtered on. The old Marlin didn't
look back.

"TURN THE BOAT AROUND AND
RETURN TO THE PIER!!"

"Morgan," the old Marlin thought back to
Morgan without turning around, "keep the
boat in sight at all times. Follow our wake."

"Okay," Morgan thought with a small leap so his parents could see he was still with them.

"And don't leap anymore."

Morgan shimmy-shagged about two feet under the surface of the water, sneaking his head out of the water every so often to see what was going on. The air bubbles from the wake danced and popped around his bill as he followed the boat.

"THE COAST GUARD HAS JUST BEEN NOTIFIED. YOU WILL BE STOPPED AND BOARDED. RETURN TO THE PIER NOW!!"

The old Marlin would not stop.

"RETURN TO THE PIER IMMEDI-ATELY!!"

Morgan stopped swimming for a moment and watched the commotion back on the pier. It already seemed very far away. The police and doctors were jumping into their cars, doors were slamming, sirens were squealing, and Morgan was bobbing happily in the wake of the little boat.

"Come on, Morgan!" shouted Spaceman.

Morgan dove beneath the surface, fell in behind the boat, and headed toward the Inlet.

CHAPTER THIRTY-ONE

THE WATER TURNED MURKIER as Morgan swam along. On both sides it was a dark greenish brown, and below him it was black.

"Why's the water so muddy?" he thought to the boat.

"This is a channel," thought Spaceman. "It's used by a lot of boats, and that keeps the bottom churned up. Just keep our wake in sight."

Morgan followed along.

"We're going to be passing another dock pretty soon," Spaceman cautioned. "One that's being used, so stay down."

"Okay," Morgan answered, zigzagging back and forth through the wake of the boat.

"Stay close and don't go outside the wake, Morgan!" shouted Spaceman. "There are other boats around here that—"

A speedboat whizzed by Morgan's head. It slap-rapped up and down over the top of the water and disappeared before Morgan had time to turn around and look at it.

He fell in behind the wake again and stopped zigzagging.

"Listen up, Morgan," Spaceman thought off the back of the boat. "There are a lot of things we're not going to have time to teach you. Use your head!"

"Morgan, listen to what he's telling you!" His mother managed to make herself heard over the drone of the engines. "You be careful down there!"

"Yes, Mom."

"When you get to the ocean," Spaceman thought, "there will be lots of things for you to learn on your own. If you're not sure about something, just swim away. There's nothing in the ocean that can catch you!"

"Nothing?!" Morgan shouted back.

"Nothing!" confirmed Spaceman. "You can see everything around you, hear things for miles, and swim faster than anything that might try to catch you. Remember that!"

"He'll be safe?" his mother asked Spaceman.

"Once we get him into the ocean, he will be," he answered. He turned back to Morgan. "Stay down, now, Morgan. We're passing the dock."

Morgan didn't need to be told that—he could smell the fuel from the ships at the dock. It was overpowering. The diesel and oil and gas mixed together smelled like turpentine. It floated by above Morgan in small oil-slick puddles that glimmered like rainbows. As he passed closer to the dock, Morgan could hear engines rumbling, feet clunking on wood, and muffled voices yelling back and forth.

"We'll be coming into some cleaner water pretty soon, Morgan," the old Marlin shouted back.

Slowly the water turned from a brackish, muddy brown, to mustardy beige, and then finally it broke apart and filtered into patches of clean water until it turned into a crispy bluish green.

"It's going to shallow up here a bit, Morgan," Spaceman thought to him. "Keep your eyes on the bottom!"

Morgan could begin to see the bottom as he swam over it. He passed over white-sanded hills and valleys that were spotted with forests of dark, flowing eelgrass and bright, yellow-green angel hair that flagged back and forth in the water with the sway of the tide. Thousands of black-shelled mussels dotted the bottom, clinging to anything that was clingable. A spit clam spat and dug itself under the sand, leaving a puff of watery sediment raining after him. Spider crabs clawed, fiddler crabs scampered under rocks, and flounder eyes peered up through the sand like little sets of camouflaged binoculars following the traffic overhead.

"There's all kinds of things down here!" Morgan shouted after popping up. He went back under without waiting for a response, cruising the valleys and meadows of his new underwater world.

He passed under a shadow that darkened the bottom of the bay. Morgan popped his head out of the water to see what it was. They were going under a tremendous bridge that spanned the length of the bay. Cars galloped loudly by and clinkity-clanked over the metal grids that stretched overhead.

"I'm going to head out into another channel, Morgan," the old Marlin thought-yelled back. "The water will get darker again because it'll be a lot deeper. Stay close."

A kingfish swam up to Morgan.

It looked at him for a quizzical moment and then fell in alongside him. They swam along with each other for a short while, then, quick as it had appeared, it was gone.

The water underneath Morgan started to darken again. It wasn't a muddy dark this time; it was a black dark. Morgan swam up to the surface.

"We're in the channel now, Morgan," Spaceman thought to Morgan. "Anywhere in between these buoys is the channel."

Morgan looked from side to side. There were red barrels floating to his left and green ones to his right.

"It's getting harder to swim!" Morgan thought to him.

"It's an incoming tide, Morgan," thought back the old Marlin. "And it's running hard. We don't have time to wait for it to change. It's going to be hard work from here on out."

"Keep your bill down and swim shallow," Spaceman coached.

The water came at Morgan in great gentle rolls. It would ease up to him, sneak under his body, and gently lift him up. Morgan would swim with it as it did. He'd swim to the top of it, and then the bottom would drop out and he would slide back down. Another moment and it would happen all over again.

"It's like a roller coaster down here!" Morgan thought loudly as he broke the surface.

"It's the waves from the ocean rolling in," answered Spaceman. "The Inlet's right in front of us."

Morgan watched the tiny boat get tossed up and down by the powerful ocean waves that rolled underneath it. Each time one did, the front end of the boat looked up toward the blue sky for a hanging moment, until the wave rolled under the back end, and then it would plunge facefirst into the water with a splash of white spray. When it did, the back end reached toward the sky and the propellers screamed as they spun out of the water for an instant.

The boat slowed to an idle.

"We can't go any farther," cried out the old Marlin. "I'll keep her in place here as long as I can. The tide's too strong right now."

Everyone was holding on tight to the boat.

"Where's the Inlet?" shouted Morgan.

"Swim out to the side of the boat," answered Spaceman.

Morgan dove under and swam to the side of the boat. When he turned sideways to do this, the tide pushed him back about ten feet. He turned his bill back into the running water and made up the ground he had lost. He broke the surface to get a good look.

The wind whipped at his face.

There, not far in front of Morgan, was the Great Inlet.

It was about one hundred yards across. One hundred yards of crashing, whitecapped seawater that ran headlong at the small mouth of the bay and slammed into it, splashing up in huge plumes of spray. The Inlet boiled and bubbled with confused and lost little wavelets that tried to keep their heads above water, only to have bigger waves tumble down and sweep them away. Sometimes the tumult would slack off for a moment. The ocean would fall back to get a running start, then head once more for the mouth of the Inlet to begin the battering all over again.

To the right side of the Inlet Morgan saw a jetty of rocks that sore-thumbed out from the shore. The waves crashed and splattered against them in loud, booming waterfalls. To the left was a snaking white sandbar that ran out into the churning waters. A flock of seagulls screeched above, sweeping in and out among one another. Some hovered in the wind, without flapping, and watched the tiny boat.

"That's the Inlet," thought Spaceman.

"I've got to swim through that?" Morgan asked.

"Yes, you do," thought the old Marlin as he walked to the back of the boat. Morgan swam a little closer. "This is it, Morgan," he thought calmly as the boat rocked back and forth. "All you have to do is get through the Inlet. We've taken you as far as we can."

The other Marlins all crowded toward the back of the boat. Molly screamed.

"Not all at once!" shouted Spaceman, as the front end of the boat lurched out of the water. "You'll tip us over!"

The Marlins spread themselves out again, and the boat settled back down.

"We just wanted to say good-bye," thought one of the Marlins.

"Well, say it from there," the old Marlin thought back sharply.

"Who wants to go first?"

"You go."

"No, you go ahead."

"I don't want to go first."

"GUYS!" the old Marlin thought at them.

"Let's school it," thought the Marlin with the cowboy hat.

"Yes," they all thought as they schooled up and looked at Morgan. "'Bye, Morgan," they thought in unison from their deepest thoughts. "Leap for us."

"Better say good-bye now," the old Marlin thought-whispered to Morgan's parents.

Morgan's mother and father grappled along the railing and made their way, together, to the back of the boat. They held on to each other and leaned over the side. They looked wet and cold; their hair blew every which way in the wind. The blue water shone in their eyes.

Morgan swam up as close to the boat as he could. He had so much to say, but no words would come. He bobbed up and down in the water as the ocean swells ran under him and waited for them to say something. But they didn't. They looked frightened and lost. Then the words came to Morgan.

"I love you, Mom," he thought up to

them. "I love you, Dad."

His father reached his hand down toward Morgan's bill and—

"TURN THE BOAT AROUND AND RETURN TO PORT! THIS IS THE UNITED STATES COAST GUARD! RETURN TO PORT!!"

Morgan spun around. Speeding up behind him was a huge white boat with red stripes streaked across its hull. The bow was filled with orange-life-jacketed doctors and police. The boat slammed and crashed through the running tide. A siren screamed.

"Morgan," his mother shouted over the side. "Morgan, do you want to go?" His father held on tightly to her as she leaned farther out. "Do you really want to go?"

Morgan looked at the Coast Guard boat closing in on him, then turned back to all the Marlins and Molly, Mrs. Pasalaqua, and his parents. All eyes were watching him.

He nodded his bill yes.

His mother stumbled slightly with the roll of a wave. She righted herself and leaned over, reaching out her hand. Morgan swam up to it and laid his bill in her palm.

"Go," she said softly. "Go."

"Good-bye, son," his father said, clutching the rail and his wife.

"We love you," they said in unison.

Morgan watched them for a moment . . . and then he plunged under the water.

"CUT YOUR ENGINES!! THIS IS THE UNITED STATES COAST GUARD. TURN YOUR ENGINES OFF IMMEDIATELY!"

Morgan popped up along the side of the boat. The old Marlin ran quickly to where he was. He looked hard at Morgan. His face was weathered and flushed red from the wind, but his eyes—his eyes were just as clear and wild as the first time Morgan had seen him.

"Go on, now," the old Marlin thought with a smile, and then turned away.

"You can do it, Morgan!" shouted Molly.

"CUT YOUR ENGINES!! CUT YOUR—"

"Oh, shut up already!!" Molly screamed at the Coast Guard.

"'Bye, Morgan," thought Spaceman. "*Open-sea free* . . . remember?"

Morgan nodded his bill and then dove

under the water.

Just as he did, the Coast Guard cutter idled over his head. Morgan looked up and saw the white-and-red slashes of its hull bump alongside the Marlin boat. The shadows of both boats stayed locked together. He popped up to see the Coast Guard boarding the little boat.

He quietly back-shagged away. He was on his own now.

His fins trembled and his heart raced wildly.

The Inlet still lay ahead.

He swam straight into it. The tide was running hard, and it was difficult for Morgan to see where he was going. He had to keep stopping and looking above the water to get his bearings, and each time he did, the tide would push him back. A wave knocked him tail over bill and carried him back to where he had started. He broke the surface and shook his head clear.

"There it is!!" shouted a binoculared sailor looking down at him. The Coast Guard boat was directly above him. He swam away from it.

Morgan heard the engines of the Coast Guard boat go into gear. He watched as the old Marlin threw his boat into gear too and turned hard to the left. The little boat swerved into the path of the Coast Guard.

Morgan swam off and headed to the Inlet. The water churned and turned white.

"Keep your bill down," he thought to himself. "Bill down, swim shallow."

He plowed forward into the onrushing tide and swam as hard as he could, trying to catch a glimpse of the ocean beyond, but the water held him at bay. He was hardly moving at all. He rested for a moment, and when he did, the tide pushed him back farther, right under the shadow of the Coast Guard's hull.

"It's right under us!!"

Morgan took off with a flash and plunged again toward the Inlet. He swam with all his strength, but he wasn't making any headway. The Coast Guard boat was closing in on him.

Then he had an idea.

He thought he'd leap.

Morgan slammed into the rushing tide and drove himself down toward the bottom. He turned his bill up, shag-swam through the swirling waters—gathering speed—and broke through the surface, leaping high and majestical over the crashing waves.

He hung there for a breathtaking moment.

In the distance, over the roar of the surf, he heard cheers and shouts coming from the little boat that floated his family and friends. His heart soared with his body. Then he pierced back into the water.

The way out of the Inlet was to leap.

He swam to the bottom again, through the white, turned to the surface, and leaped over another set of waves.

Down to the bottom, wait for a wave, rush to the top, and LEAP!

He did it again.

Down to the bottom, wait for a wave, rush to the top, and LEAP!

It was working. Under the waves, in front of him, Morgan glimpsed something he had not seen before. Swaths of rich, vibrant colors streaked his underwater horizon, blues so deep and rich that Morgan had no words to describe them . . . windows of sky that opened and closed through the clouds of tumbling surf. They would appear through the swirling white for a moment, like a white curtain briefly blown open by a gust of wind, and then disappear again.

It was the ocean.

It was a leap away.

Morgan headed to the bottom again, farther than he had ever gone. He turned upward and swam with all his might, with every ounce of Marlin in him, he raced, he flew toward the surface, broke the water, and—*LEAPED!*—flinging, hurling, catapulting himself over the last crashing waves of the Inlet. He plunged into the water beyond, bill first, with hardly a splash.

The tide stopped pushing.

The water stopped crashing.

The waves stopped waving.

Morgan floated free in quiet waters—the ice-blue, clear-green waters of the ocean.

Around him, as far as he could see, was nothing but room to swim.

His body tingled with excitement.

Morgan shimmy-shagged in a tight circle and headed to the bottom. Deep, dark blues flashed by him, blues bluer than any blue he had ever seen. He swam harder. There was no limit to how far he could swim. Deeper and deeper he swam. The bottom never came. He pulled his bill up and stopped for a moment, gently suspended in the calm of the ocean. He finned quietly, turning himself in all directions.

All around him was choice.

He glanced up at the rippled blue above. The sun was now a little pinspot of white that shimmered on the surface. He headed for it. He swam as hard and as fast as he could. Then he swam faster. The waters rushing over his body roared through his senses. Ever faster . . . up and up he flew. The shimmering circle of the sun grew bigger as Morgan soared upward. He pointed his bill at the center of it, gave one last shag of his powerful tail, and exploded through the surface of the ocean, shattering the sea into a billion tiny shards of glistening water drops that flew across the sky like a burst of diamonds.

Morgan hung in the air, for minutes it seemed. A rush of excitement thrilled through his body. There, before him, as far as he could see, straight out to the horizon where blue meets blue, was the unimaginable expanse of the sea.

Joyfully Morgan tumbled back into the ocean . . . and leaped away.